13 Haunted Nights

EMILIA ROSE

Hey Mom and Dad! If you're reading this dedication, please skip to the next page. I promise that you really don't want to see what this book is dedicated to.

Honestly, you should probably put the entire story down now anyway. It'll make things way less awkward during Thanksgiving.

.

Please, I'm begging you.

.

Last warning!

.

.

.

To all the fucked-up monster porn that I watched for inspiration <3

VANDERSON VAMPIRES

CONTENT WARNING: ELEMENTS OF DUBCON,
PRIMAL PLAY, BLOOD PLAY, VAMPIRES

Clutching the golden cross that hung around my neck, I walked underneath the black metal archway and onto the Vanderson's Property. Every year on the last night in October, a nun was sacrificed to the monsters of this land to satisfy their hunger until the next year.

This year, the head priest in my village had selected me.

A large bat swooped down from the archway, his wing grazing against my shoulder. He flew ahead toward the castle, his body disappearing into the large dark clouds that laid overhead.

Heavy tears trembled in my eyes, but I continued forward in order to protect my loved ones back home. No nun had ever returned, and many of their bodies had been dumped deep in the woods, found with bite marks on their necks, their bodies pale and bloodless.

I followed the zigzagging path up the slight sloping mountain to a gray Victorian-style castle with red lights glimmering from the top rooms. When I spotted the line of nuns standing outside of a side door, I clasped my cross tighter.

This was for my sisters. This was for my people. This was for my family.

We stood in the freezing cold for hours, waiting to be checked in and categorized by blood-type. "Next!" a tall burly man with pale skin and dull fangs shouted at me.

With my hands clasped together, I scurried into the building and out of the cold for the first time today. My lips were numb, my fingers shaking. I stood in front of him, stared at the stone floor, and shivered.

I didn't want to be here, but I had no other choice.

He stalked around me, looked me up and down, then gave a dissatisfied grunt. I closed my eyes and muttered a prayer, hoping that somehow I would live through this torture.

"Finger," he ordered.

Once I presented my index finger to him, he drew a sharp claw across it and cut my skin. A bead of blood dripped out onto my flesh. He scrunched his nose and shoved me toward an old steel door.

"First commoner of the group!" he shouted. "Bring her to the back."

Another vampire snatched my neck and steered me down a long hallway lined with metal cells. Nuns filled the cages, some dressed in their traditional garbs while others had had their skirts cut short or their tops ripped off so their tits hung out.

Some vampires walked up and down the corridor, scanning the cages for their next meal. I pressed my lips together and hoped that because my blood was common, nobody would want me.

Or maybe... that'd just be worse for me. Because then someone would suck me dry and kill me in one night. While nuns with tastier blood might live to see other days because the vampires didn't want to lose them.

I spotted the nun sacrificed from my village last year sitting in one of the less common blood type rooms with fang marks all over her neck. I balled my hands into tight fists by my side and swore to myself that I wouldn't cry.

But I... was a goner.

I wouldn't live until morning. I would be bled dry tonight by a commoner who couldn't control himself. I would have done my duty to the village and to my family.

"Walk," the vampire behind me growled.

After stumbling down the hallway, we walked into a back room that didn't have anyone else in it, which only confirmed my growing theory even more. Commoners didn't stay around that long.

He bound my wrist to a chain and shut the door. I sat on the cold stone floor and chewed on the inside of my cheek, a terrible habit that I thought I had quit for good during Lent last year.

Hours later, the same burly man who checked me into the Vanderson's Property walked into the room and sat at a metal desk, picking up a pencil to write some notes.

The large bat that I had seen earlier on my walk onto the estate swooped into the room and perched on the windowsill, his wings outstretching and his body morphing into one of a vampire.

Dark messy hair. Pale skin. Black tattoos that crawled up his arms and torso.

He folded his wings back into his body and leapt off the windowsill and into the room. Closing his eyes, he inhaled deeply and walked toward me. "A gift for the night of the monster."

The master nodded. "A gift indeed, but there are others you should see first in the other room." The master placed a hand on the vampire's shoulder, guiding him into the corridor.

When they disappeared, I huddled in the corner and grasped my cross, praying that God would save me, hoping that he would *hear* my prayers in this forsaken place.

"Have a taste," the elder said, voice traveling. "And take your pick."

A moment later, they reappeared back into the room, and the vampire strode toward me. He paused inches from me, still completely and utterly naked, his... dick hanging out for me to see.

I had never seen one besides in drawings and had only heard about them through the sisters' gossip. Sinful heat grew between my legs. I clutched my cross and prayed that God would forgive me.

After forcing myself to peel my gaze away from him, I looked back into his hazy eyes and swallowed hard. My nipples hardened, aching for me to touch them, to tug on them through my tunic.

"She's new," the vampire said, his tongue gliding across the prick of his fang. He reached out his arm and brushed his fingers across the center of my chest, nearly touching my golden cross that would burn him. "The nun from Carco Village?"

"Her blood is common," the burly vampire said. "None of your brothers or sisters want her. And I doubt she'll do much for you. We have a better selection up front. Nuns from the other village with rarer blood and bigger tits. Why don't you—"

"I want her."

"But—"

Before the man would mutter another word, the vampire sped through the air and pinned the burly man against the wall with ease. He moved so fast I could barely see him.

"I want her," he growled through his fangs. "Do I make myself clear?"

"Y-Yes, Sir Alaric."

Once the burly man unhooked my chains from the wall, he handed them to Alaric Vanderson. He led me through a larger door and into a main hallway. Vampires glanced over at us, grimacing when they saw Alaric–a royal–tugging me along with him.

But I was his food for tonight.

He probably wanted to bleed a nun dry to celebrate the holiday.

While I had heard whispers back home of the vampires' play-room—where they sucked blood and fucked nuns together in a club-like area—he led me to the bottom floor and into a bedroom.

I hesitantly stepped into the room and gazed around at the canopy bed sized for a king and the couches made from the riches of fabrics. I had never seen things like this before. Not in my poor village.

Alaric shut the door behind me and slowly stalked closer. Inches from me, he paused and stared down at me, a slight haze over his piercing eyes. My mother and father had always taught me to never stare into the eyes of a vampire, but I... couldn't help myself.

If I was going to die here tonight, if God would not spare my life, then I wanted to look into the devil's eyes and show him that I wasn't afraid... though I really was.

Instead of ripping down my tunic to expose my neck and suck me dry, he brought his fingers up to my face and drew them across my forehead, then down my nose, across my cheekbones to my lips, his touch soft.

"What are you going to do with me?" I whispered.

He didn't answer.

He trailed his fingers down my chin to my throat, then he touched the cross that hung on top of my breasts through my garb. His skin sizzled, and he yanked his arm away, sucking the tips of his fingers into his mouth and cursing.

"Don't you know that if you touch a cross, you will burn?" I asked, brows furrowed together. I gently tugged his fingers toward me and stared in horror at the burn forming on his skin. "Do you have any ointment to treat it?"

"It will treat itself," he said, pausing. "Why do you care?"

I stared from eye to eye, unable to see into the man's soul like I had done to so many other men and women who attended church. I could always tell if they were good, bad, believers or not.

But he was right. Why did I care? He was about to kill me.

Still, I... couldn't help myself.

"Why did you touch my cross?" I asked, refusing to answer his question.

"I didn't see it."

"It's laying right on my chest."

He paused once more. "You've seen me transform into a bat."

"And?" I whispered, glancing down at the skin reforming where the burn had once been. My eyes widened at how... easy and how quick vampires could regenerate and heal. If only humans could have that power.

All the sick men and women I saw daily could live to see another day.

A low, dark chuckle escaped from his lips. "Do they educate you in Carco Village?"

"Excuse me?" I said, taken aback. "Are you insulting my intelligence?"

"Yes," he said, lips pulled into a soft smile. "What's your name?"

"That is not how you talk to a lady," I said in a sudden burst of confidence. I crossed my arms and stared up at his sculpted face. "I would never give my name to any devil like you."

"If I was a devil, I would have ripped your cross off you by now and have forbidden you from wearing it in my chambers."

"You're not going to make me take it off?"

"The cross?" he asked, lips curled into a smirk. "No. Because no god will save you from me." He curled his hand around my throat. "One day, you'll take off the chain and realize that the only gods are the ones who live in this castle."

I swallowed hard and stiffened.

"What's your name?" he repeated.

"I'm Daphne," I whispered.

"Daphne," he said, tracing my throat with the pads of his fingers. "Say it again."

"Daphne."

"Daphne, have you ever heard of the expression, 'Blind as a bat?'"

"Y-Yes."

"Where do you think that expression comes from?"

I dropped my gaze and stared at his wrist just below my chin. "I'm not sure who has come up with such lies, but bats are not truly blind. I'm not that uneducated, Sir Alaric."

"Sir Alaric, so formal," he hummed. "You're correct. Most bats aren't fully blind but, if you couldn't tell, I'm not like most vampires, Daphne. My tastes are a bit... different."

"You're blind?" I asked, eyes widening.

Maybe this was God's way of saving me.

But while the thought of trying to escape crossed my mind, I couldn't shake the feeling of pity. A vampire from the royal family who ruled over this continent couldn't actually see any of its beauty.

"My family doesn't allow me to have *food* in my quarters, because when they discover I'm blind they try to escape the estate." He drew his fingers up the column of my neck. "But the last human who tried to leave me... I bled dry."

My eyes widened, and I pressed my thighs together. "I won't leave. I... I promise. My village selected me to satisfy the monsters who live here. I can't go back to them without fulfilling my duties."

"They sent you here to die for them," he said. "Not to fulfill any sacred duty to a higher god. We don't send humans back unless we're done using them for their blood."

Swallowing hard, I clasped my hands together as realization finally set in. All this time, I had contemplated why they had sent me, knowing deep down it was to save themselves. No priests and no monks ever made the journey.

Only nuns.

"Why'd you choose me?" I whispered.

"What do you mean?"

"My blood isn't rare. And the burly vampire downstairs was right. My body isn't one to lust after. I belong with a common vampire, not a royal, Sir Alaric. You should take another nun to please you this holiday."

His hand tightened around my throat, and he pinned me to the wall. "I will take no one other than you," he murmured. "You're mine. You've always been mine."

"Always been yours?" I repeated. "Wh-What does that mean?"

Instead of answering me, he clicked his tongue and walked to the window. After popping it open, he turned back around and clicked his tongue once more, turning in my direction.

"Come," he ordered.

I walked toward him and stared out into the chilly fall night.

"Now, run."

"R-Run?" I whispered.

His full lips curled into a smirk. "I like to play with my food before I devour it." He drew his thumb down my lips. "Blood tastes better when it's laced with adrenaline." He chuckled quietly. "Run."

Throat dry, I climbed out of the window and sprinted through the woods without him having to tell me a third time. I pumped my legs hard and tugged up on my tunic to sprint more easily, branches and twigs scraping my legs.

Suddenly, Alaric flew over the trees above me, the wind from his wings rustling the leaves. I inhaled sharply and continued running. God had given me a chance to live, to escape the monsters... and if Alaric wanted me to run, then I would run as fast and as far as I could.

Faster. I pushed faster. I pumped my legs faster. I ran faster. And longer. And harder.

Not caring what was ahead of me, because it couldn't be worse than a mansion full of vampires who wanted to suck me dry.

My feet slipped off the edge of the cliff, my back scraped against the rocks at the top, and then my body fell through the air. My cross clattered against my chest, and I gripped it tightly.

If this was God's way of saving me from those monsters, then so be—

Alaric swooped down, his wings gliding through the air, and caught me in his powerful arms. He pulled me to his naked chest and glided through the air, his wings pushing us higher and higher and higher.

We flew to the top of the cliff, then—just when I thought he'd put me down—he flew with me back to the castle. Instead of landing on the windowsill as he had before, or even on the roof, he hovered over the castle with me in his arms and my legs straddled around his waist.

He took my chin in his hand. "I'm going to show you who you belong to from now on, Daphne. The monster that you're now bound to. The man who will suck your blood every night for eternity."

My tunic rode up my legs already, but he swept his hands underneath it and scrunched it up to my hips, his fingers wrapping around my white undergarments.

"I took a vow of chastity," I whispered, heat gathering between my thighs.

"And tonight you're going to break it," he murmured, his lips inches from mine. "Atop the Vanderson's castle. For the entire world to see. You're going to be begging me not to stop."

Wetness pooled between my legs as he ground himself against my underwear. Nobody had ever... touched me there before but his... cock... I bit back a whimper. It was throbbing against me.

And it felt so good.

"So good," I whispered.

He moved his fingers skillfully around my clit through my underwear, pushing me closer and closer to the edge. I grasped onto his muscular shoulders and stared into his eyes.

Though he couldn't quite see me the way I saw him, he had complete control of everything that happened. I couldn't run. I couldn't hide. And I definitely couldn't stop the ache in my pussy.

"Reach down between us," he ordered. "And touch it."

Gulping, I dropped my gaze to his chest, then to his huge cock between us. I lowered my hand and clenched, my fingers slowly wrapping around his thickness. It was so... so big.

"This is..." I whispered, wrapping my hand around it tighter. "... wrong..." I moved my hand up and down his length faster, pussy tightening. My breathing quickened. "So wrong."

"You're getting so wet for me," he murmured against my ear, swooping a finger around the waistband of my underwear and tearing them off me completely. "We're going to take care of that."

Still swinging his wings behind himself to hold us up, he positioned himself underneath me, the head of his cock rubbing against my wet entrance. I sucked in a breath, nerves racing through me.

Slowly, he pushed himself inside me, filling me inch by inch, and broke my vow for good.

"Do you know why we allow nuns to keep their tunics on?" he

hummed into my ear, his face buried into my neck and his fangs running up and down the ridges of my collarbone until they landed right on my sweet spot.

"Why?" I whispered, clenching.

"Because it gives us vampires a rush when we get to fuck a woman who had sacrificed her life to a fake god, who had pledged to live a holy life free from sin and from pleasure." He stilled deep inside me. "To feel her squirm in ecstasy for the first time. To turn her into a cock-loving little whore."

With his hands all over my body, I threw my head back and moaned softly. This was so wrong, but his voice... his filthy mouth... I couldn't stop myself from clenching around him.

After wrapping a hand into my hair and pulling it back, he peppered hot kisses all over my neck, his fangs trailing across my artery. I curled my fingers into his shoulders and slightly bucked my hips to meet his rhythm.

Sinner.

I had become a sinner in God's eyes. I had broken my vow to him.

Alaric gently groped my breasts through my tunic and over my hardened nipples. When he took my nipples between his fingers and tugged, I couldn't stop a low moan from escaping my lips.

I slipped a hand into his hair and tugged softly, completely blinded by the ecstasy. Euphoria rushed through my body, making me tingle everywhere. He dipped his head and sucked my nipple between his teeth through my tunic, biting enough to make me squirm.

"More," I begged, an indescribable sensation rising in my core. "Please, more."

He sucked on my nipple harder, his hands groping and kneading my ass. I dug my fingers into his shoulders, the pressure too intense in my core. Alaric slammed himself into me deep and hard.

"Pray to your god that you don't get pregnant when I bury my cum inside your tight little hole," he growled into my ear.

"P-Please, father…" I bit my lip to hold back a moan, my words escaping me. This was far too wrong for me to ask for forgiveness. My people, my family, my sisters had kept this away from me for far too long. "Please, don't make me pregnant."

"Fuuuuck," he groaned, pounding into me. "Just like that."

His fangs trailed up and down my throat, right above my artery. I tensed and waited for him to slip his teeth inside me, for him to suck my blood just as he had promised.

"Do it," I whispered, my judgment clouded by pleasure.

"Not yet," he murmured.

I threw my head back and moaned. "Please!"

He slammed into me harder, my clit pressing against his taut abdomen repeatedly, sending me higher, pushing me closer. And when his fangs pricked my flesh, I screamed. Wave after wave of pleasure rushed through me, my mind hazy. He sank his fangs into my neck—the pain almost non-existent as the euphoria shot through my entire body.

He pulled me closer to him and stilled deep inside my pussy, sucking hard on my neck, his lips latched onto my skin right above my collarbone. I curled my toes and lolled my head back more.

Letting him take complete control of me.

And when I saw stars, my grip on him weakened, he slowly pulled away from me and licked his bloody lips. His chin was covered in my blood, and his eyes… God, his eyes were pitch black. Another wave of pleasure rushed through me.

He lowered us to a landing at the top of the castle and set me down. I sat on my knees, his cum drooling from my pussy. He licked another bead of blood off his lips and walked over to me, feeling around my face until he reached my chin.

"Ask for forgiveness while your cunt is filled with my cum."

I clasped my hands together in front of me and stared up at Alaric who looked more like a god than any man I had seen before as cum dribbled out of my pussy. "F-Forgive me, father, for I have sin-n-ned."

LOVE CHEMICAL

I pumped my legs as fast as they would go and glanced over my shoulder. Nine zombies staggered after me through downtown New York City, their bodies decaying and the smell of rotten flesh trailing me.

God, what was I thinking?! Releasing that goddamn chemical to attempt to change the zombies' behavior? This is worse than five days ago! I'm going to fucking die out here!

Whimpering to myself as a cramp twisted my stomach, I drove my legs further, my sneakers slapping against the pavement. Plastic pumpkins and cloth ghosts decorated the city. The outbreak had hit nine days before Halloween.

Nine fucking days ago, and this city was already a ghost town.

My shoe string caught on a loose bumper of an abandoned car, and I tumbled forward onto the road with a thud, attracting the attention of other nearby zombies.

Before I could stand, hands were all over my body, touching, groping, kneading my flesh. I screamed at the top of my lungs, heart pounding so hard in my chest and tears pouring from my eyes. Everyone I loved had died this way, and now it was my turn.

Claws dug into my skin, tearing it. I desperately tried to scurry to my feet, but there were far too many undead monsters for me to regain my balance and run away. I prepared for the first bite—because from what we've seen, the first was always the worst.

But instead of teeth claiming my body, hands were. Mouths were.

Cocks were.

I flipped over onto my ass and stared in horror at the soulless men, desperate to rub themselves off on me. I sucked in a sharp breath, heart pounding. In my experiments at the lab, I had seen crazy shit but nothing like this.

What the hell is... going on?

Gaze drifting from the surrounding zombies to the others nearby, I spotted two creatures shoving their dicks into the eyes of a carved pumpkin. Others grinding against plastic Halloween skeletons.

Holy shit.

The chemicals had really done something. The zombies were evolving.

Evolvi—

A zombie slapped me in the face with his cock. Another pulled my lips apart and rammed his dick into my mouth. Both hands on the back of my head, he slammed himself deep into my throat, forcing me to gag every single time.

I widened my eyes, tears filling them, and pushed on his thighs. But two others grabbed each of my wrists and wrapped my hands around their cocks, thrusting themselves back and forth in my grasp.

Spit rolled down my chin and dripped onto my chest. Zombies tugged at my clothes, their long nails ripping into the thin material and tearing it off in strands. My tits bounced out of my shirt, and two hands wrapped around them from behind, groping me.

Another pushed my breasts together and shoved his dick between them. My spit rolled down my cleavage, making it wet for his cock. Each one took their turn ruining my throat, gagging me, fucking my mouth dry.

I dropped one hand between my thighs and pressed it against my clit to stop it from aching. My pussy was pulsing, drooling, dripping with anticipation. These zombies were undead monsters with their dicks hanging out of their ripped and bloody clothes, speaking in grunts and growls instead of coherent words.

This was... exactly what the chemical was supposed to do.

Exactly how the zombies were supposed to react.

Moaning around a cock, I slipped my hand underneath my jeans and massaged my clit. Pressure grew between my thighs, the pleasure building up inside me. I curled my toes and cried out on the zombie.

Grunts, groans, and growls drifted through the abandoned city street.

My throat tightened. The need to breathe became overwhelming. But I didn't want to stop. I had really done it. The team back at the lab had really done it! We changed the zombies' behaviors, their DNA.

One grabbed a fistful of my hair and ripped it back. The dick fell out of my mouth as I was forced to stare up at the zombie behind me. He pulled my head back even further and shoved his cock into my mouth, his heavy balls smacking me in the face with every thrust.

More hands moved up and down my body, clawing at my waistband in an attempt to pull them down. I unbuttoned my pants and let the zombies yank them off me. Multiple sets of hands, mouths, and cocks pressed against my bare legs.

I spread my thighs and cried out in pleasure when one shoved themselves inside my cunt. Pumping in and out. Pounding into my tight, wet, drooling hole.

Heat rushed to my pussy. They fucked me like they were famished, starving, hungry for a wet pussy. Cocks thrusted in and out of me. Spit rolled down my chin and onto my bouncing tits. Undead hands trailed all over my skin, grasping at my human flesh.

Another pinched my nipples between his fingers, and I fucking lost it. My entire body trembled. Wave after wave of pleasure shot through me, my mind numb, my mind *lost*. I screamed out and jerked my thighs up.

"God!" I moaned. "We did it... We really did it."

SLAVE OF THE CIRCUS
CONTENT WARNING: SLAVE, CLOWN

I sat in a small dog cage in the back of a dark tent, naked and shivering. Around me, other slaves laid in the cages, some small, others large with multiple women in them. Most of us had been trapped here for weeks, waiting to be bought. To be owned.

Buyers never came into the tent without a disguise, without a mask or make-up to cover their faces. It wasn't because there was shame behind owning a personal slave, but the owners made it a sick game.

He was no different.

Black smudged eyeshadow covered his eyes. Harsh black lipstick stretched from one of his cheeks to the other in the shape of a wicked, menacing grin. White face paint covering all the skin he had bared, even his hands.

With a black cane that looked to be more part of his costume than for actual use, he walked around the cages of tired and naked slaves, who pressed themselves to the cold metal bars just to be noticed. Usually, I inched forward too.

But I didn't have the energy tonight.

Instead, I sat in the back of the cage, my stomach growling

from lack of food and my limbs too weak to move a couple inches. I closed my eyes and bit back a whimper—the master of this slave ring didn't like any kinds of moans or whimpers from his pets.

Especially with potential buyers walking around.

Like owners usually did, the man in the clown makeup passed me without a glance.

Three cages down, he stopped in front of a petite woman. I covered my tummy with my arms, loathing the fact that men chose all the other slaves first, and closed my eyes. I had been so hopeful for so long.

Now, it seemed so useless.

Something clattered in front of me, and I snapped my eyes open.

He stood at my cage, running his cane along the bars. "This one."

"Are you sure that you want her?" Master Ruicher said. "You haven't even checked the entire selection yet, sir. We picked out—"

"This. One."

Ruicher rummaged through his pockets and pulled out a key ring. After shuffling to a key labeled eighty-seven, he stuffed it into the keyhole and opened my cage for the first time since he had thrown me in here.

"Come out," Ruicher ordered.

I scooted to the edge of the cage and stared up into the darkest, most heartless eyes I had ever seen. Of a clown who had lost all sense of comedy. Of a monster in need of a slave. Of a man looking to become a master.

"Come to me," he ordered.

After using the cage to hoist myself to my feet, I walked on shaky legs toward him. Besides the pieces of bread that Ruicher tossed into our cages every other day, I hadn't eaten anything for nearly a month.

Ruicher pulled out a metal collar from his large coat pocket that zapped a slave whenever they disobeyed their masters and handed it to the man. The clown tossed it aside and took the chains that bound my wrists together. "She won't be needing that," he said, scanning my face. "She won't disobey me."

CHAINS BOUND AROUND MY WRISTS, I sat in the red and white stands inside the circus tent and pressed my thighs together as the performance finished. It had been seventeen days since Crimson bought me. Seventeen days of circus stunts and being scared for my life that he'd die and I'd be sent back to being a slave.

Every morning, he brought me to the circus so I could watch the daredevil stunts he pulled, driving a motorcycle in a large sphere cage with a handful of other guys. Yet every night, he walked home with me and unbound my hands so I could wander free inside his small apartment down in the city.

While he never had given me a chance to see his actual face yet, I had seen the scars that decorated his back muscles and the burns from the fire stunts. I had grown closer to him—almost too close, too comfortable for my own good.

The ringmaster opened the metal globe and released the bikers, dismissing them for the night. As Crimson had requested, I sat off to the side and didn't stand to greet him like the other slaves did their masters after the show.

Instead, I peered at him from across the tent. He stared back at me, leaning against his bike as he chatted tensely with the ringmaster. I nervously glanced between the ringmaster—who reminded me of Ruicher—and Crimson, chewing on the inside of my cheek.

A couple moments later, the ringmaster stormed out of the tent.

Crimson cocked his brow at me. "Come," he said, voice echoing.

My eyes widened, because he had never invited me inside the arena before. But I stood and hurried over to him, my chains clattering against each other. His body was covered in sweat, his tattoos glistening.

Hands snaking around my waist, he picked me up and sat me on his lap on the bike. I inhaled sharply, never having been this close to him before. "Wh-What are you doing?" I whispered, nervous that someone would see.

He pulled a key out of his pocket and unlocked my chains here.

Which he had never done before.

"Hold on tight," he said.

"H-Hold on to what?" I whispered, staring down at his sweaty, taut body. My gaze dropped even lower to the way I straddled him, my pussy nestled against his crotch, the heat growing between my legs.

"Me," he said, starting the bike.

Which was forbidden too.

A slave couldn't be on the equipment they used here. And the bikes were circus property, forbidden to leave the tent. But by the way he revved the engine... It didn't seem like we were staying here.

"We're getting out of here," he said. "For good."

When the bike lunged forward, I clutched hard onto him, my arms wrapping around his shoulders and my front pressed against his. He hit the accelerator, speeding up to exit the tent, the tires lifting off the ground.

I buried my face into the crook of his neck, wincing at the thought of crashing. But he steered the bike through the streets, down thin alleyways, and out of our small city with ease, speeding up the entire time. Wind whipped my hair back.

We drove and drove and drove for what seemed like hours until he finally parked on the side of the road and turned off the bike. I lifted my head off his shoulder and glanced around at large steel gates in front of the most massive mansion that I had ever seen.

"What is this place?" I asked.

"My home," he said.

"B-But your home is an old apartment back in the city," I whispered. "This is a mansion."

And the biggest estate I had ever seen.

Instead of moving me, he leaned back on the bike and stared. I peered over at him, then down at how close I was to him. I quickly jerked back—because slaves should never be this close to their masters unless the master orders them too.

But he placed his hand on the small of my back and pulled me toward him once more.

Eyes as dark as the night, he didn't say a word to me. The heat grew between my thighs again, the thought of him in that cage of death, the fire stunts he had pulled off with ease way too many times in the past few weeks...

Part of me didn't even believe he was human.

"What are you?" I whispered.

"You shouldn't ask questions you don't want answers to."

"I want to know."

He grasped my chin, gaze darkening. "A monster."

But to me, he was a fucking savior. A man I would do anything for.

Willingly.

"I've waited to touch you for weeks now," he murmured, hand clasped around my jaw. "Weeks of watching you undress in that spare bedroom, watching to see if you'd attempt to escape while I left you alone. Most slaves would've taken the chance. Why'd you stay?"

"Because you're nice to me," I said, voice trembling. I dropped my gaze to his shoulders, then to his chest, then to the front of his pants, his bulge. God, he was so close. "Right?"

"You're trembling already," he murmured. "I've barely touched you."

I pressed my thighs together.

He slipped his hand under my waistband and pressed his long fingers against the front of my underwear. "You're ruined for me," he mumbled, his head dipping into the crook of my neck. "So fucking ruined."

I bit my lip to muffle a whimper as he dragged his fingertips against my slit through my underwear. Even if I wasn't a slave, I couldn't fight back. I couldn't tell him no, that I didn't want it, that the thought of him didn't make me wet.

Because I'd be a liar.

Watching me carefully, he slid his fingers underneath my underwear. I stiffened and widened my eyes, the heat exploding between my legs. Nobody had ever touched me there before tonight.

After tracing my clit, he dropped his fingers lower and pushed them into me.

"Ride my fingers," he ordered.

"I-I don't know how," I whispered.

With his free hand, he grasped my hip and moved my ass up and down on him, forcing me to ride his digits, my thoughts slipping away and my mind emptying for the first time in a long time.

"Just like that," he murmured, slowly releasing me. "You're doing so well."

Like he showed me, I moved my hips back and forth, the pressure rising in my core. The mere friction of his palm against my clit drove me mad. He placed his lips on my soft spot, right below my ear, and sucked on the skin. A wave of pleasure rushed through me.

He trailed his hand up to the zipper of my shirt, pulling it down and letting me fall out of it. Grunting, he groped one of my breasts and squeezed it hard. My nipple rolled around his rough palm, sending another wave of heat to my core. My pussy tightened around his fingers, the pressure too much to handle.

"You're going to come for me, little mouse," he murmured.

He curled his fingers inside me at just the right angle, sending me over the edge. My body shuddered against him, my mind foggy, and my limbs numb. He pulled his fingers out of me and sucked them into his mouth, his eyes growing even darker behind all that makeup.

After licking his lips, he scooped me into his arms and walked with me onto the estate, into the house, and to the couch, his dick growing harder against my backside. When he sat me down on my hands and knees, he slid off my pants and underwear, undid his jeans, and pushed them down to his knees.

I stared with wide eyes at his huge cock, my pussy growing even warmer. He slapped his dick against my ass, once and then twice, then he slipped it to my pussy lips. A wad of spit dripped from his mouth to his throbbing, veiny cock. With his thumb, he massaged the spit over his head, then rubbed it against my clit from behind.

Swallowing hard, I clutched onto the couch cushion and bit my lip to hold back a moan. He continued to drag the head of his cock against my slit and grabbed my waist with his free hand, bending over me to place his mouth on my shoulder.

"You're mine, little mouse."

Crimson lined the head of his cock up with my entrance and slowly slid into me. My pussy clenched even harder around him as he stretched me out. He slipped his arm around my waist and rubbed my clit.

As he pounded himself into me from behind, I squeezed my eyes closed to focus on the pressure building quickly between my legs. His mouth was all over my neck, peppering wet and desperate kisses up the column of my throat.

Ramming his cock into my tight hole, he grunted. "Let me come inside you."

My pussy tightened around his enormous cock.

Usually, masters didn't ask for permission. But God, hearing those words come out of his mouth–like I was the one with all the control–it made me feel a certain type of way. I arched my back so he could thrust into me deeper.

"Pleas–"

"Yes," I cried, wave after wave of pleasure rushing through me. "Come inside m–"

Before I could even finish my sentence, he slammed his dick into me and groaned. I threw my head back and screamed out in pleasure, wave after wave rushing through my entire body. My legs trembled, my mind numbing.

"You asked me what I was," he finally murmured, pulling out of me while I still came down from the indescribable orgasm. His cum dripped between my pussy lips and onto the couch underneath me. He dipped his fingers into my cunt again and shoved his cum back inside me. "Soon, I'll put you back into chains, lock you to my headboard, and fuck you senseless every waking moment of the day. I'm going to be your worst nightmare, little mouse."

FOUR MASKED WOLVES

Dressed in a tiny black latex costume that *hid nothing*, I curled my arm around Gaian's elbow and stepped onto the sidewalk that led to Maxine's Halloween party. Maxine lived alone in a house that her ancestors had passed down through the generations. Sitting on the outskirts of Durnbone, the gray stone house stood three stories tall against the foggy night, covered in cobwebs and fake spiders, blood and gore.

"Sina!" Maxine shouted as we approached the doorway, as if she had been waiting for us. She threw her arms around my shoulders and pulled me into the house, her gaze lingering on my scantily covered body. "You look so sexy!"

"Maxine!" I said, covering my breasts with my hands, not enjoying the sudden attention brought to me by her. My four mates might've dressed me tonight, but I didn't want the attention from any other species or people besides them. I had too much other shit to worry about than wandering eyes. "Can you lower your voice?"

"No, bitch." She grinned, shutting the door behind my wolves. "You're sexy as hell."

Calder grabbed my hand. "Thanks for the invite, Maxine."

"Of course!" she beamed, her boyfriend whisking her away.

Three of my mates, Calder, Gaian, and Darius, disappeared into the crowd to chat with people they knew around Durnbone, while I stayed glued to Thayer's hip. They had dressed me in this sexy assassin outfit with a face mask and everything.

And the number of guys who kept peeking my way was making me... *uncomfortable.*

In the best way possible.

"Can I take off this mask?" I asked Thayer, squeezing his hand to stay close.

More and more people began crowding into the room, the air becoming heavier with body heat. Hundreds of scents flooded through my nose, and I desperately needed some fresh air. This mask wasn't doing shit right now.

After taking one long look at me, Thayer smirked. "No."

"Why? What does it—"

Before I could even finish my sentence, something extended from the inside of the mask, slipped all the way into my mouth, and was shoved down my throat. My eyes widened with tears as I gagged on the object and grabbed onto Thayer. I tried to open my mouth to speak, but I couldn't get out a single word.

Instead of helping me, Thayer grinned even wider, wrapped an arm around my shoulder, and pulled me closer to him to whisper into my ear. "Tonight, you're our cute, little cumslut who's going to take our cum anywhere that we want you to."

I let out some muffled words that even I couldn't understand.

"Do you remember the trinket shop downtown that we visited last week? Well, we found a little toy that we can use on you," he hummed, strumming his fingers over my shoulder and making the hairs on my arms raise. "A toy that lets us fuck your pretty mouth whenever and whenever we want as long as you have this mask on."

Thayer wrapped his arm around my waist and guided me through party as Calder, Darius, and Gaian used that toy to fuck my throat. And I could do nothing and say nothing without globs of spit and drool running down my throat.

Demons that Thayer knew walked up to us and directed questions at me, but I kept my lips sealed and let Thayer do all the talking. It wasn't like I could actually say anything in return. And while I knew Thayer didn't like any of these guys, he loved watching me be a mess.

"Look at your filthy little mouth," he said, using his finger to wipe some drool running down my chin once a couple demons left us by the bar alone. He moved his finger lower to trace the cock buried deep inside my throat. "Do you think anyone has noticed yet?"

For a moment, whoever was buried in my throat pulled out to let me breathe. I inhaled sharply, my chest rising and falling in this slutty little outfit. "I... I don't know," I whispered, heart racing and cheeks flushing. "I hope not."

But truthfully, I believed *everyone* had noticed me being face fucked.

"Well," Thayer growled, pulling out a hair elastic from his pocket and fisting my hair in his hands. "Let's make sure that everyone does." He pulled my hair behind my shoulders, letting only a few strands slip out. "After tonight, everyone is going to know not to mess with what's ours."

"You're psyc–"

Before I could finish my sentence, someone slipped their dick back into my throat. I gagged on it and grabbed Thayer's hand, tears welling up in my eyes again from the sudden movement.

"Open your mouth wider," Thayer ordered, gently pushing the hair out of my face.

I opened wider to breathe, but the only thing that came out of my mouth were sloppy, spit-filled squeaking and gagging sounds as my guys used my mouth. Thayer wrapped his arms around me from behind and ground his cock against my ass.

"Everyone is staring at you," he murmured into my ear.

Glancing around the party, I realized that everyone really was staring at me. Demons, wolves, vampires, witches, and even some majestic faeries that rarely attended Durnbone parties. I moved back against Thayer to hide myself, but he was having none of it.

"You look like my easy, little slut tonight," Thayer growled into my ear.

A small whimper escaped my throat, and I pressed my thighs together. I loved being used and abused by these four guys who I trusted more than anything. I loved their filthy mouths and the way they wanted me to dress up like their whore for tonight.

After whimpering again, I turned around to face him and wrapped my arms around his shoulders. As spit and drool rolled down my chin and my makeup smeared from the tears slipping from my eyes, I furrowed my brows and begged him with my expression to fuck me.

I needed him inside me so badly. I needed something inside me. Anything.

He wrapped his hand around the front of my throat, thumb rubbing across the dick in my throat and his knee gliding up between my legs. "Is Pretty Bird getting desperate for it? Hmm? Does she need to relieve herself here in front of everyone?"

Layers of drool ran down my throat. "Mmhmm."

He ground his knee against the latex material that covered my pussy. "Get yourself off on me. I want you squirting all over me, making a mess of yourself in the middle of the party, in front of all your friends."

Gripping onto him tighter, I swallowed around the cock and glanced around the party. While most people had gone back to dancing and having a good time with each other, some were still watching me intently. And I knew that Calder, Gaian, and Darius were all here somewhere watching me too.

I must've looked so desperate and needy, because I couldn't stop myself from dry-humping Thayer's knee. I glided my clit back and forth, over and over, driving myself higher and higher.

The pressure built up, my pussy tightening on nothingness. I gripped Thayer's shoulders and stared up at him through wide eyes, my face absolutely ruined from all the face fucking tonight.

"Is that all you fucking have, Pretty Bird?" Thayer growled, eyes shimmering demon-red. "You got a throat full of cock and you're still a horny little whore for us tonight." He slipped a hand under the latex material that covered my pussy and cupped my cunt. "You want this? Hmm?"

Whimpering, I nodded.

"Then you'll fucking beg me to take you right here."

I gripped onto him tighter and begged, but my words came out gargled and full of spit. Someone slipped their cock all the way down my throat, fucking me harder and faster and deeper until their warm cum filled me all the way up.

When they pulled out, my mouth was full with so much cum that it drenched the mask I wore and ran down my throat and between my cleavage, making my tits glisten under Maxine's dim living room light.

"Please," I pleaded with Thayer. "Please, fu–"

Another one of my guys slipped their dick into my throat too to fill me up. I gagged and gargled on his cock, bucking my hips back and forth against Thayer's long, thick fingers. Gods, I needed it so badly. So fucking badly.

Heat crawled up my body, slowly igniting it in what felt like flames. It was the same desperate, flaming heat that had made me into a wild mess the other day with Calder. Now... it was coming out with Thayer too. I wanted–needed–to be bred, to be full with cum.

Thayer slipped onto a bar stool behind him and pulled me onto his lap, my back against his chest and his cock pressed against the latex material covering my cunt. He pulled up my skirt just enough and ripped off the latex panties underneath it.

"You're a fucking mess," he growled against me. "A sloppy, slutty mess."

"Please," I begged, words still muffled. "Please, fill me!"

"Fuck, Pretty Bird," Gaian growled to my right, hurrying over to me without trying to even hide the bulge in his pants. He pushed through a small crowd, grabbed my arm from Thayer and tugged me into a hallway that Maxine and I used to play hide and seek in when we were younger.

After Gaian thrust me into a coat closet, Thayer walked in and shut the door behind us. I curled my toes at the thought of them both taking me while Darius and Calder took turns using my tight throat for their pleasure.

"God, I can't fucking wait my turn out there," Gaian said, shoving me onto my knees and whipping out his cock.

Thayer sat back against the wall, pulled me onto his lap, and spread my thighs further apart in order to give himself better access to my pussy. I moaned on the cock in my mouth, cheeks flushing and pleasure rushing to my core.

Thayer rubbed his cock against my glistening pussy. Pushing it between my pussy lips, he teased my clit by rubbing and slapping it with the head of his cock. I whimpered and moved my ass back on his lap to hover over him.

"Ple–"

He shoved himself inside me, his cock filling my tight hole. I curled my toes, letting whoever was inside me fuck my throat until I could barely breathe. My legs trembled slightly, and I squeezed my eyes closed.

Gaian stepped closer to me and shoved his cock between my cum-covered cleavage. His cock disappeared between my breasts for a moment, then the head appeared at the top, my drool dripping onto it. He groped my breasts through the latex material, rolling my hardening nipples between his fingers and tugging harder with every thrust.

Pleasure shot through my body, and I clamped down on Thayer's cock with my pussy. Thayer growled into my ear, shoving himself deeper and faster into me. My pussy continued to pulse over and over on his dick, the feeling on him inside me almost enough to send me over the edge.

"Fuck, Sina," Gaian growled, pressing my tits together and thrusting up one last time between them. As the head of his cock emerged from between my tits, his cum squirted all over them, covering my cleavage and even my throat.

At the same time, cum filled my mouth and layers of it spilled down my chest and between my breasts too. I screamed out in pleasure when I could finally breathe again, my legs trembling hard in Thayer's hands.

"Please give it to me, Thayer," I moaned.

"Beg like the filthy whore you are."

"Gods, please," I pleaded, moving my hips back and forth on his cock. "I need someone's cum inside me so badly. Thayer, ple–"

Before I could finish my sentence, Thayer smacked my clit with his large hand and I came undone. Pleasure rushed through my body, wave after wave of ecstasy making me feel so fucking good. Thayer stilled deep inside my hole and came against my cervix, as deep as he could get.

THIS ONE SHOT **has been made into a full length novel. It releases on wide retailers in 2023 and is currently available to read on Patreon.**

WITCH TOYS

Potion bubbled in the black steel cauldron in my bedroom. I stirred the contents with a long wooden spoon and inhaled the scents of lust. Thousands of witches had tried and tested this spell throughout the years, but nobody had ever gotten it right.

Not until today.

This was my sixty-first attempt at solidifying potion and giving it a purpose.

After grabbing a pair of mittens, I took the cauldron off the fire and placed it near my bed to let it cool, to shape, to form. As the purple chilled into a slimy structure, I pulled back the blankets on my mattress and prepared for tonight.

If this worked—*if it truly worked*—tonight would be the best night I have had in a long time.

Fifteen minutes later, I returned to the contents and dipped my bare hands into the gooey purple mix. Excess potion dripped off the object, allowing the phallic body to finish forming.

My lips curled into a smile as I hopped onto my bed with the twiddling object.

I sank down into my mattress and breathed out a sigh of

relief. After all these years, all these attempts, I had finally done what no other witch has done before. I created an object whose sole purpose was to fuck, a dildo that had a mind of its own.

The object leaped from my hands and plopped down onto the mattress. Like a fish out of water, it flopped back and forth; the head dribbling precum onto my sheets. I peeled off my underwear and spread my legs.

It floated between them and brushed its head against my entrance. Then within a moment, it slammed into my drooling pussy. I screamed out and threw my head back, sounds of pleasure escaping my throat.

Pressure grew in my core as the heat radiated through me. My arms flailed from the pleasure, a loud moan escaping my mouth. I desperately tried to control myself, but I accidentally knocked over the *Lover's Potion* on my nightstand into the cauldron, the potion mixing with the rest in the large black bowl.

Bubbles boiled and popped in the pot. Steam formed above the rusting steel. The cauldron shook back and forth until it eventually tipped over and spilled all onto my old oak hardwood floors.

Cursing to myself, I glanced over the edge of the bed while the dildo still rammed into my pussy. A glob of pink slime slithered out of the pot, tentacles writhing through the air. My eyes widened, and I scurried up to the headboard, wondering what the fuck that was.

Never in my life had I ever seen such a monstrosity. Not even at the witch academy.

Dildo plunged deep into my cunt, I scrambled to the other side of the bed to grab my staff, so I could neutralize whatever kind of concoction I had accidentally stirred up. But one tentacle rolled around my ankle and yanked me back to that side of the bed.

I grasped onto the bed sheets, the dildo still thrusting into my pussy.

With its tentacles, the glob pulled me off the bed and into the air. The mass couldn't form beyond a mere puddle on the floor. Instead, it matted to the ground and tugged me in any direction that it liked. One tentacle gripped my right ankle, another wrapping around my upper thigh. A third ripped the dildo from my pussy and snapped it right in half.

"No!" I shrieked. "All my hardwor—"

Before I could finish my sentence, one appendage slipped into my mouth, another into my pussy, and a third into my ass. All at once. I cried out in pain and pleasure, my toes curling from the ecstasy rushing through me.

My head lolled backward, my spine arching. I opened my mouth wider, letting the tentacles use my body however they'd like. I didn't know what kind of spell I had stirred up, what kind of monster I had created, but I couldn't seem to care at this point.

They all pumped in and out of me at varying speeds, different lengths. Some rough. Others slow.

Another wrapped around my breasts, squeezing them together, the wet tips twirling around my nipples and leaving a thin trail of pink ooze. And one more slid between them to fuck my tits, the little pink suckers leaving red circles on my soft flesh.

"M-More!" I cried, words muffled.

All the tentacles thrust into me faster, bringing me closer and closer to the edge. I screamed out in pleasure, my legs trembling as wave after wave of pleasure rushed through me. My mind went fuzzy, blank.

But even when I finished, the tentacles continued to use me. Not stopping once.

I quickly came to a second orgasm. Then a third.

Then I began thinking that they... that they wouldn't stop. That they would never let me go. Never give me a break. This giant glob of goop was about to fuck me to death.

MUMMY GOD

CONTENT WARNING: DUBCON, BONDAGE,
GODS

"I really don't think we should do this," I whispered to my sister, Valeria.

We had snuck onto private property that had been rumored to hold tombs of men who lived four millenniums ago. When I was just a child, our parents had warned us to stay away from the Ivywood Residence in October because the men inside the tombs came alive and would whisk us away to a faraway land.

Of course, it was all a rumor.

Many old friends had snuck onto the land, found the tombs, and tried to open them up on Halloween night, just for the fright. But the stones were too heavy to move and the residence itself was filled with spiders and cobwebs, not any ancient undead gods.

Still, it was creepy as hell.

I would much rather spend the night handing out candy than this.

"No turning back now," Valeria hummed, using her phone's flashlight.

I grumbled to myself and followed her down the cobblestone steps that had been chipping away through the cold, harsh winters. Eying the door at the end of the staircase, I chewed on the inside of my cheek. *Why am I getting a bad feeling about this?*

Once we finally landed on the last step, she pushed on the door but it didn't budge.

"Oh well," I said, nervously glancing over my shoulder. "We should get going."

"We didn't hike for the past two hours for nothing," she said. "Help me."

"Valeria, come on. Let's just go home."

"Help me," she said.

Knowing her, she wouldn't leave with me unless I, at least, tried to open the door with her. So, I rolled my eyes and planned to *act* like I was giving it my all with the push, but would really just tap the door and tell her it was too heavy.

"Come on," she said again, leaning against the door with all her might. "Push with me."

I laid my hand upon the door so lightly, making it creek open. My eyes widened, heart pounding. *W-What was that?* I barely touched the thing. Surely, Valeria could've done that by herself...

"Yes!" Valeria cheered, pushing the door open even further and stepping into a tomb.

A freaking tomb!

Why wasn't she scared shitless like I was? Who the hell explored tombs on Halloween night? And why had it been so easy for me to help her open that door? It looked like it weighed four-thousand pounds.

"Don't fall behind!" Valeria called from inside, her voice echoing down the hallway.

I stepped into the tomb—because I sure as hell wasn't going to stand alone in the dark outside by myself—and followed Valeria's phone light that must've been ten yards ahead by now and dimming every second.

"Valeria, please wait," I begged, moving my legs faster. My

foot hit a lone rock sitting in the middle of the walkway, and I fell forward. Before I could hit the ground, something snagged me from behind.

A piercing scream left my throat, and I twirled around to see a piece of cloth that hung from the ceiling had gotten twisted around my upper arm, the tattered cloth so strong that it had caught me before I face-planted.

After placing a hand over my heart, I blew out a breath, regained my composure, and ripped the cloth off me. When I turned back to follow Valeria she had disappeared completely and had left me in a pitch-black tomb all by myself.

"Valeria!" I shouted, placing one hand on the stone wall and using it to guide me down the hallway. The wall dipped in, and I stepped into a new room with a small lit torch fastened in a wall sconce.

Weird.

I grabbed it and ambled around the tomb, staring at the enormous sealed burial coffin in the center, surrounded by gold, amulets, diamond-encrusted dishes, and silver jewelry. Everything looked so... old. And expensive.

Walking over to the walls covered in paintings, I drew my fingers across the symbols that I had never seen before. They weren't Latin spellings or any type of hieroglyphics from Ancient Egypt that I remembered from high school.

When I was finally done being creeped out, I turned away from the wall and headed back toward the door. But when my gaze landed on the burial casket, I froze and widened my eyes. It wasn't open when I walked in...

Was it?

"I've been waiting for you," a man said from behind me.

Another piercing scream escaped my throat, the torch falling from my hand and rolling to the corner of the room. I took off toward the door and tripped over some antiques. My body smacked onto the hard stone floors, the skin on my palms tearing and covered in blood.

"So clumsy," he hummed from behind me.

I glanced back at a mummy barely illuminated by the flickering flame in the room's corner who now stalked toward me. I desperately pushed myself up to my hands and knees, needing to make it to the door now.

But two pieces of cloth wrapped around my ankles.

When I looked back, the linen around the mummy's body was unraveling and wrapping around my legs. Like magic, it folded around my calves, then slithered up my knees to my thighs and tugged my body back down to the ground.

Still, I used all the strength I had left to crawl across the dirty stone floor with my hands toward the exit. When I was inches from escaping, the door slammed closed, separating me from the rest of the tomb and from Valeria.

"Valeria!" I screamed.

With the cloth wrapped around my ankles, he pulled me all the way up into the air—upside down—until we were face to face. Piercing green eyes glowed through the dark spaces between the cloth. "The only name you should scream is mine."

Man, I was scared shitless, but his eyes. Damn his eyes were mesmerizing. I had never seen anything as captivating before. This wasn't a man. He couldn't be. He had survived down here for centuries alone, without food and water.

My mouth dried. He had to be... a god.

I shook my head, not wanting to believe it. I had grown up Catholic and had since sworn off all religion because I didn't believe in that crap, but there was no other explanation for this. This mummy had come back to life.

"I haven't seen a woman in many years," he murmured, the cloth falling from his head and revealing a sculpted face, his jaw so strong, cheekbones sharp. "You've come onto my estate, awoken me and my brothers, and now... you'll pay for it."

"P-P-Pay," I whispered, the blood rushing to my head.

"Open your mouth."

And while I never obeyed *any* man, my mouth fell open. He lowered me a couple feet until my face was inches from his cloth-covered cock. I pressed my thighs together and stared at the bulge pinned to his leg tightly in cloth. Heat gathered between my legs.

Holy—

Slowly, the cloth unraveled enough for his dick to slip out. Drool dribbled down my face, my cunt salivating at the sight of his huge cock. I whimpered when the head brushed against my lips. He pushed it inside my mouth and hit the back of my throat long before even half of him was inside me. I gagged on it and attempted to pull my head back, but he slammed his hips forward and forced me to take every inch of him, his balls slapping against my forehead.

From above, he used his cloth to spread my legs. More linen wrapped around my waist, slipped between the buttons of my shirt, and popped them off. He dipped his head between my thighs, his warm breath on my pussy.

I moaned out in pleasure on his enormous dick, spit and drool rolling down my cheeks while he fucked my face. I opened my mouth wider, my throat squeaking every time he thrust up into it. I wrapped my arms around the backs of his thighs and pulled myself closer to him, so I could take more.

When he placed his warm mouth on my clit, I cried out in pleasure around him. He flicked his tongue across my clit, over and over and over, lapping up my juices, eating me like a feral fucking animal.

I didn't know how he had possessed me to do this, but I couldn't stop.

He grunted—the mere sound making my legs shake. "I

haven't tasted anything so good." He buried his face between my legs and continued to eat my pussy better than any man had. "I'm fucking starving."

Eyes watering, I forced all of him down my throat and swallowed, choking myself on his huge dick. He grunted again and slammed his hips even harder against my mouth, his balls smacking me in the face.

"More," I moaned on him, my words muffled. "Please, give me more!"

After pulling away from my cunt, he loosened his grip on the cloth, thrust his hips back, and set me right side up. Two more strands of linen wrapped around my elbows and bounded my arms behind my back, circling around my limbs until they were completely covered.

"Spread your legs," he ordered, tugging me closer until I sat helplessly in his arms.

He lined the head of his cock up with my entrance, took my chin in his hand, and slammed himself into me as his lips pressed against mine. I cried out into his mouth, something so devilish pulling me to him.

He had a grip on me—a mental one, not just physical—that I couldn't escape.

My pussy tightened around his dick, the pressure rising in my core. I curled my toes and wrapped my legs around his cloth-covered waist to tug him even closer. He pounded up into me, spreading and stretching my pussy.

He drove into me over and over, his tongue in my mouth and his hands all over my body. "I've been waiting for you," he murmured against my lips. His hands dropped to my ass, and he squeezed. "I've been waiting so long for this."

He trailed kisses down the column of my neck to my collarbone, then pulled my arms back until I sat at a forty-five degree angle, my tits on full display to him. A chill ran through the room, my nipples hardening. He sucked one into his mouth and bit down.

Pleasure surged through my body, and I screamed out. My limbs went numb, my mind light. I collapsed in his arms as the ecstasy rolled through me. He sucked a bit more on my nipple and pulled back, thrusting in me once, twice, and then for a third time.

After he spilled all his cum deep into my pussy, he pulled out of me and dropped his gaze, watching as his cum dripped onto the stone floors. I finally could tear my eyes away from his piercing green ones, and his hold on me suddenly vanished.

My heart raced. "Valeria," I breathed, scrambling in his arms. "I need to go find her. To get out—"

"Your sister doesn't even know you're here with me," he said suddenly, a mist clouding over the room. An image of my sister and I exploring the tomb appeared through the haze. They walked to the exit and out into the night as if I had been with her the entire time.

"H-How is this possible?" I whispered. "What did you do?"

"Whisked you away," he murmured. "You should've listened to your parents. This tomb is filled with monsters, not men, who have been long awaiting the arrival of a woman who will help us ascend back into the world. *You*."

PSYCH WARD

Sex deprived.

I snapped my shoulders back and forth, desperately trying to escape the straitjacket that Doctor Holland had stuffed me inside of while I slept two nights ago. After spending the last three months convincing me to finally check into the Covenpeak Hospital for my sex addiction, he had betrayed me.

Betrayed me!

"Let me out of here!" I screamed, tears streaming down my cheeks.

Heat grew between my thighs, taunting me. I needed to touch myself. Badly. It had been forty-eight hours since my hands had been between my thighs, since I had been rubbing myself off against the metal bars of my bed frame while Holland watched me through the double-sided mirror.

"You'll fucking regret this, Hollan–"

Before I had any more time to protest, the bulky box television with two antennas directly in front of me turned on. A flurry of static appeared on the screen, followed by two naked bodies grinding against each other.

"Please, stop it!" I cried, knowing that I wouldn't be able to last another night of porn. On the screen, a woman was being filled by three men in one hole. As the pressure built between my thighs, I slashed my shoulders back and forth. "I can't handle this anymore!"

The door opened, and Holland walked into the padded white room.

"I thought they didn't put patients in straitjackets anymore!" I cried. "Let me out!"

"Patients?" he chuckled darkly. "Did you actually believe my little lie, Tamara? Did you really believe I worked at Covenpeak Hospital? At *any* mental institute for that matter?" He stalked into the room. "Maybe I'm not even a therapist."

"You're a bastard!" I growled. "Let me out. Now!"

"If you had kept up with your behavior," he said, drawing his fingers up the column of my neck and then tucking some hair behind my ear, "you would have hurt yourself. I had to restrain you for your own good."

"How is this for my own good?!" I screamed.

I was a crying, sopping mess. My pussy was aching so badly. I wanted out. Now.

"I'm here to give you the therapy that you so desperately need," he murmured.

Slowly, he loosened the straps that bounded my feet together until it came undone. Then he undid the next strap up my legs, then the next, and the next until he undid the one around my knees and I could finally move slightly.

"I bet your pretty pussy is begging to be filled," he murmured, rubbing his fingers over my clit through the straitjacket. Pressure rose in my core, threatening to push me over the edge already, and he barely touched me yet.

When he pulled away, I whined. "D-Don't stop-p. Please, I need it!"

He walked to the door and pulled out a metal service cart with medical supplies on it. After wheeling over the cart, he grabbed a knife from it. "Now, don't move," he warned, cutting up my left pant leg to my pussy. Then he did the same with the right pant leg to gain complete access to my drooling cunt.

When he pressed the blunt side of the blade against my clit, I whimpered, so desperately wanting to move my hips back and forth. My pussy was aching to be touched, to be filled. He rubbed it slowly, pushing me closer to the edge.

I balled my hands into fists, my nipples taut.

"My pussy," he hummed, watching me while he picked up the pace with the knife. "Mine."

"Y-Yours," I cried out in pleasure, loving the blade.

I didn't care what he pressed against my clit. It could be a gun for all I cared. I just wanted to be touched all over, to come, to crawl onto his enormous cock and ride him all night long. My gaze flickered to the TV where a man was fucking a woman in a full nelson, and a moan escaped my mouth.

"Your pussy is soaked," he noted.

He drew the tip of the knife from my clit to my hips, then gently dug it into me. I winced in pain, the pleasure quickly fading. He shoved two fingers into me to satisfy my hungry pussy —the pain completely disappearing because I had something inside me—then proceeded to dip the knife into my flesh until it sliced through my skin.

"You're doing so amazing," he hummed, pumping his fingers inside me. "So good."

He carved the letter 'R' into my hip, followed by H. His initials.

I hadn't known him for long, but before he had tricked me into coming here, he had taken me out on a single candlelit dinner down by the river. All night I had thought it was the most magical thing in the entire world—and about how he promised to fuck me in the bathroom afterward.

He stabbed the bloody knife into the wooden chair between

my legs, then pulled his fingers out of me—leaving me empty yet again. "Make yourself feel good," he said. "You're going to need it once I'm finished with you."

With my arms bound, I lifted my hips enough to hover over the knife's handle, then I sat down on it and moaned out in pleasure. He walked back to his metal cart to prepare something, but all that mattered now was that I was full.

So full.

I bounced on the knife's handle and moaned again, my mind numb and my every need satisfied. Up and down and up and down, I fucked myself on the handle and wished that it was even bigger. I wanted to be stretched out. Stuffed full.

"More," I moaned. "I need your cock."

He smirked over at me, his eyes hooded and dark. "We're going to see how much your pussy can take," he said, seizing a speculum from the metal cart. He glanced at the knife. "Off." When I scurried off the handle, he tossed it aside onto the concrete floor and drew the cold metal up my inner thigh, then pressed it against my sopping entrance and pushed it into me easily. "Most patients would freeze up right about now, but not you..." He chuckled. "No, not you."

After thrusting it all the way inside me, he twisted it open. Once. Twice.

Then he paused and glanced up. "How do you feel?"

"F-F-Fill my pussy!" I cried. "Please!"

Crouching in front of me, he reached under the metal cart and pulled out an eight-inch long dildo. My pussy tightened at the thought of having it inside me, and I spread my legs even further. He slid the dildo between the speculum and into my pussy.

I cried out in pleasure, eyes rolling back in my head, as he pounded it into me.

"Bigger! Give me something bigger!"

He pulled the pussy juice covered dildo out of me and set it on the metal tray. After adjusting the speculum to spread my pussy wider, he retrieved another dildo, this one at least ten inches and three inches thick. When he shoved it inside me, I screamed out and came all over it.

"More," I begged. "More. More. More. Give me more!"

He thrust it inside me, pounding it into my tight hole. I placed my feet on the chair and did the best that I could to thrust myself deeper and deeper onto it whenever I could. I loved the way it felt inside me, the fucking girth.

When he pulled it out of me, I whimpered. "N-N-No."

"Don't worry, sweetheart. I have another for you."

He set the dildo on the metal tray and grabbed a third dildo. After opening my speculum to the widest setting ever, he set the twelve inch dildo at my entrance and slammed it into me. My body jerked back and forth, another orgasm ripping through me.

"I've never had a patient quite like you," he murmured, thrusting it in and out. "You can take any size that I give you, and you still want more. It doesn't matter how big, how thick. All your sloppy little pussy wants is to be filled with cock."

"M-M-More!" I cried. "I want to come again."

"No more for you," he said, pulling the dildo from me and leaving me completely empty.

The speculum still spread my pussy apart, and I clenched around it as hard as I could. "Please, give me more or let me out! I can't handle the torture of being locked up like this any longer. I need to come."

"You already have," he hummed. "Many times."

"You don't understand."

"I completely understand, Tamara. You're a hungry whore for cock." He stepped closer to me and drew his fingers up my inner thigh, chuckling low. "Did you think that this was all to please you? You're just my test subject. Nothing more."

"Let me out!" I cried. "Please!"

"We're going to fill your cunt with cum that has been harvested from other patients," he murmured, uncovering a gallon jug of white liquid on the metal cart. "And we'll see how your slutty little pussy reacts to it. I'd bet your hungry cervix will swallow it right up."

THE GRAVEYARD
CONTENT WARNING: SKELETON

I stood before the iron arbor gate at the entrance of the Black Bones Cemetery. A gray fog laid over the gravestones, the light from the full moon illuminating the heavy clouds. I sucked in a breath and stepped into the realm of corpses.

For only one night a year, Death could walk in the world unnoticed, his black cloak and scythe almost common amongst the children trick-or-treating and adults heading to Halloween parties. He didn't need a disguise, not that he could even wear one anymore.

We could go anywhere in the world, but tonight he had asked me to meet him here.

Thousands of years had passed since he took his rightful place as the King of Death, the King of Darkness, of Hell itself. Thousands of years since the love of my life had been forced to leave me. Each year, we had one night together. One night that I would forever cherish.

"The goddess of life," cold lips murmured against my neck from behind, the roll of his tongue so familiar. He brushed his boney fingers up my arms, sending shivers down my spine. "Just as beautiful as I remember."

I twirled around to see the man—the god—dressed in a black cloak behind me, wielding a scythe, the metal blade glinting under the moonlight. "The King of Death," I hummed, brushing my fingers across his tattered black hood to try to see his face.

Darkness swarmed around inside, his body nothing more than bones and mist.

"Do you want to know why I chose this graveyard this year?" he asked me.

"Why?"

He took my hand and led me to the rows of stones, then stopped at a small one that barely reached my mid-shin. A man who was just as weak as he was poor, the grave of a human whom I had found solace in this past year.

His name, Fredrico, was carved into the gravestone.

"Do you remember him?" he murmured against my neck.

"I could never forget the men and women that you take from me," I whispered, running my fingers across the carvings in the stone, the rock grainy against my fingertips. "The souls of my creations that you steal daily."

"But Fredrico is special," Death said.

"He was never as special as you," I whispered. "Nobody could be."

The hood of his cloak fell down, the skull of a man I once knew staring back at me. Every year, more and more of his flesh had melted off into the hellish pits where he lived. And this year was the first when he was nothing but bones.

"You shared a bed with him," he said.

"As if you haven't had another woman in your bed since last year," I said, staring back.

He might've been bones dressed in a cloak, but he was still the sexiest damn man I had ever laid my eyes upon. And by far, the most powerful being alive. He had the power to destroy life just by lifting his finger.

"The last woman I was inside of was *you*," he murmured, brushing his knuckles across my cheek and then down my chin. Then he wrapped his hand around my throat. "And I'll be inside you again. Tonight. On top of Fredrico's grave."

"You're a sick man," I whispered, warmth exploding through my core.

"I'm no man," he said, shoving me down to my knees and snatching my chin, forcing me to look up at him. "I'm a god, and gods are worshiped. Now bend over your lover's grave like a good girl for me."

Wetness pooled between my thighs. I flipped over and rested my forearms on the cement grave, my ass in the air and my pussy aching for him. I had gone an entire year without him inside me, a year of measly hookups that hadn't given me any pleasure at all.

He dropped behind me, his skeleton hands all over my ass, grasping my waist, traveling underneath my dress. "All the men I've taken from you," he said, his hand made of bones moving up the front of my neck. "I've stolen their souls, so they can't have you. They were too fond of your beauty, of your vigor. And you, darling..." he murmured, breath fanning my skin. "... are mine."

His mist darkened behind me, extending out into black appendages. One slithered around my throat and slipped into my mouth, entwining with my tongue. Another wrapped around my hair and pulled it back, so I could watch Death take me however he wanted.

"You're mine," he declared. "Say it."

"Yours," I murmured on the mist, my words muffled. "All yours."

Two more gusts of mist wrapped around the tops of my thighs and spread them apart. He slipped his arm around my waist and trailed his fingers from my navel to my slit, rubbing his boney fingers across my swollen clit.

"The next time you want me," he said. "You come to this

grave, spread your legs, stuff your pretty fingers inside your hungry cunt, and scream my name."

I moaned, spit dribbling down my chin and dripping onto Fredrico's headstone.

"No mortal has ever made you this wet, has he?" he murmured into my ear. "And I have barely touched you yet." He moved his fingers across my clit faster. "I remember the days when I could draw my tongue across your body and taste every inch of you, especially this messy little cunt."

My legs trembled.

"Poor baby is shaking for me." He cooed. "Are you going to come already?"

Pressure rose in my core. I furrowed my brows together and curled my fingers around the gravestone, moaning on his appendage. He rubbed my pussy harder, faster. "Mine," he growled. "You're all mine." He smacked my clit, and I screamed all over him. "Mine. Mine. Mine. Mine. Mine. Mine. Mine."

When he pulled his hand away from my clit, he slithered his appendage between my pussy lips and toyed with my aching, pulsing pussy. My eyes rolled back in my head as I impatiently waited for him to fill up my tight cunt.

"Oh baby, you're drooling all over yourself." He ran a bony finger across my chin and swiped up some spit. "You look like such a desperate, dirty slut for me." He pressed the head of himself against my pussy, stretching it apart further than any human man could. "As soon as I shove myself into you, you'll remember why you're mine."

With every inch he pressed inside me, I tightened around him more and more. All I had wanted since last Halloween was finally here. He grasped my chin and turned my head, forcing me to stare up into those dark pits.

His eyes had once been such a lively hazel brown, but I preferred them this way. I had always and would always love the man he had become. No amount of darkness could ever change that.

In one thrust, he slammed himself all the way inside me. I cried out in pleasure and stared up at him, gently pulling the appendage from my mouth and placing my lips on his boney face. "I fucking love you more than you'll ever know. I'm yours, Death. All yours."

He pounded into me harder and faster than Fredrico ever could, his thrusts long and deep. I clutched the gravestone with both hands to hold myself steady and moaned into his mouth, my pussy clenching around his enormous cock. I screamed out in pleasure, an orgasm ripping through me.

"Say it again," he said, slowing his thrusts.

"I'm yours, Death."

He rubbed his fingers across my clit once more. "Tell me you love me."

"I love you," I whispered. "I will love you even when the flowers dry out, the humans go extinct, and my ability to create life ceases to exist. I will love you even when you decide that watching me sleep in a casket all year long is far more peaceful for you than only seeing me for a few moments once every year."

"Don't you say that," he murmured against my lips, thrusting into me even slower, his hands seizing my waist and his fingers curling around my hips. "I could never take the life of the woman I love. I would wait for eternity to spend one day with you, my sweetness."

Hot tears welled in my eyes. When he pulled out of me, I turned around and stared up.

"I don't want you to go," I whispered, grabbing onto his hand that was nothing more than decaying bones. Tears raced down my cheeks. "What if the next time I see you... you're even lesser than what you are now? What happens when there is no more of you for me to touch?"

"One day there won't be," he said. "But I will still love you. I will still visit you. I will still be with you every October." He pushed the tears away with his thumbs. "And you'll still create life, because when you do... it's fucking beautiful. Do you understand me?"

"Yes," I sobbed.

When I finally calmed down, he took my hand. "I must go now," he whispered. "Will you be okay?"

No.

"Yes, I'll be fine," I whispered. "I always am."

But really, this past year... had made me not want to live. I had done everything to keep myself going, even stooped so low as to let another man touch me. I didn't know if I would make it another year without him.

He placed a kiss on my mouth, then seized his scythe. I stood as tall and as strong as I could, giving him my best smile so he wouldn't know that he had such a powerful hold on me, that this was slowly killing me.

Then he turned away from me and walked to the black iron gate at the exit of the graveyard, disappearing through the deep fog. And when he was gone for good, my legs gave out and I doubled over the grave once more.

"Don't go," I sobbed. "Please, don't leave me here alone!"

SUMMONING SEX DEMONS

CONTENT WARNING: MONSTER

"Alright," Jada yawned. "I'm calling it a night."

Lightning struck through the sky, thunder cracking overhead.

"That's enough *spookiness* for me," Mikayla said sarcastically, following Jada out of my bedroom. "Three hours of Ouija board and witch curses later, and we can't even communicate with a simple ghost!"

Jada tugged on one of her brown coiled curls and frowned as Mikayla slumped her shoulders forward and trudged down the hallway. "Happy Halloween!" Jada teased. "I can't wait to decorate for Christmas tomorrow!"

"Happy Halloween to us," Mikayla grumbled from down the hall, then slammed her door.

Jada rolled her eyes. "She'll get over it. You need help cleaning up?"

"No," I giggled. "I'm good."

"Alright," she grinned, her brown eyes glimmering in the moonlight. "Night."

"Night," I said. I picked up the ouija board from the floor and shoved it into the back of my closet for next year, then gently shut the closet door. Mikayla loved Halloween with a passion, obsessed over ghosts and ghouls, and had even memorized a plethora of spells from when we visited Salem, Massachusetts last year.

While I didn't particularly believe in the mystical, I played along with her since she was my bestie of seven years. If she were anyone else, I would've laughed in their face for even suggesting that we play with a ouija board on Halloween.

Another roll of thunder crashed through the night, and the lights in my bedroom went out. I crawled into my bed and underneath my covers, snuggling up with my blankets and shutting my eyes. I waited to hear Mikayla's shouts through the house that this was a sign, that a spirit was trying to communicate with us.

But she didn't say a word.

I opened my eyes and sat up in bed, leaning over to stare out my window. Light blazed out from Mikayla's bedroom next to mine. The hair stood up on my arms. Why had... Why had only my power gone out?

Deciding that it was nothing, that I was just hallucinating, I relaxed back into bed and closed my eyes. Mikayla was just getting inside my head now. We had been at it for hours tonight. I must've started believing it myself.

Stupid, River.

My floorboard creaked. I snapped my eyes open.

"Mikayla, if you're trying to scare me, it's not working."

The hell, it isn't. I am about to piss myself.

Heart pounding, I glanced at the bedroom door which was shut. I shifted my gaze around the room to see the closet door—which I knew I had closed—now open ajar. My mouth dried. *What is going on?*

I scanned the room and found nothing. No one. This was my imagination.

"Stop letting her get inside your head," I whispered to myself, grabbing the blankets and pulling them up to my chin. "There are no such things as ghosts. There are no such things as ghosts. There are no such thing as–"

Someone brushed their fingers against my ankle that stuck out from underneath my blankets. I shrieked and sat up in the bed, heart pounding inside my chest. I pressed my back against my wooden headboard and reached for my lamp, hoping to God that it'd turn on.

Nothing.

"Wh-What's going on?" I whispered.

"Relax," a man with the deepest voice purred into my ear.

A shiver ran down my spine. I snapped my head in the direction of the voice. Nobody.

The fingers suddenly slithered around my shoulders, then down my bare arms, pushing the blankets away. Goosebumps raised on my skin, and I felt paralyzed to the damn spot. Two hands disappeared underneath my shirt, the large knuckles making indents as they traveled up to my breasts.

My nipples hardened, the warmth growing between my legs. When he flicked my nipples with his fingers–which felt more like claws–I threw my head back and moaned. I didn't know why it felt so good–*There was a stranger in my bedroom!*–but I couldn't stop the pleasure from surging through me.

"W-Who are you?" I whimpered, watching the indent of his knuckles against my shirt.

Waiting for him to flick my nipples again.

"Innocent little human," he hummed, hands traveling *down* my body to the waistband of my pants. "You don't even realize what you and your friends summoned tonight, do you?" He let out a low chuckle that annihilated me. "*Who* you and your friends summoned tonight."

He dipped his hand between my legs and cupped my wet, throbbing pussy. A set of lips brushed against my collarbone, the man's warm breath fanning my bare neck. Another breathy moan escaped my lips.

Moonlight flooded in through the curtains, illuminating the monster in my bed. Sharp teeth, red-tinted skin, large black horns. I didn't even know if I would scream if I could. My mouth was dry, my pussy *wet*.

A demon who must've been twice my size laid beside me and slipped his large fingers inside my cunt. I reached between my legs and seized his wrist, the pressure quickly building up inside my pussy.

"J-Jade! Mikayla!" I shouted, heart pounding.

"Call for them all you want." He used his free hand to lift my chin, so I stared directly into his pitch-black eyes. Inside their reflection, I could see into Jade and Mikayla's rooms and watched them get fucked and fondled by other large demons too. "They're busy."

"W-What are you going to do with me?" I whispered.

"Everything you desire."

Before I could ask any more questions, he flipped me over so I laid on my stomach. With his knees on either side of my legs, he pinned my hips to the mattress, leaned over me, and grabbed a fistful of my hair, tugging up on it. "Tell me what you desire."

I opened my mouth to speak, but all I could do was moan when I felt how huge his cock was. He ground it up and down against my ass and between my thin silky pajama shorts. I curled my toes and whimpered, my ass bucking back against his like I didn't have control of my body anymore. My pussy was sopping wet and aching to be filled.

"What do you desire?" he asked again.

"For you to ruin me."

The only words I could summon out of my throat. *Ruin me.*

Ruin me hard. Fast. Deep. I didn't care.

"Good girl," he cooed into my ear from behind, then released my hair and smacked my ass cheeks hard. "Get up onto all fours. I can't promise that I will be gentle with you. My cock is going to stretch out your tight little human cunt like no dick ever has before."

Heat rushed through me. I followed his orders and pushed my ass back until I sat on all fours in front of him, my breasts falling out of my tiny tank-top and my pussy juices soaking through my bottoms.

He rested his forehead against mine, lifted one of my hands off the bed, and forced me to wrap it around his large horn. I arched my back and gripped the ridged edges with my palm. Then he did it with my other hand.

"Don't let go," he said, sprawling one hand across my chest and ripping off my shirt at the seams. My tits bounced around, my nipples hardening from the sudden chill. I tightened my grip on his horns and clenched.

Instead of ripping off my pants with his brute strength, he pulled out his cock and pressed it against my pussy from outside my pants. He rubbed it back and forth the silky material, pressing harder and harder against it each time.

I curled my toes, waiting for him to shove himself into me. He rested his hands on my ass, pulling the material apart until the seams stretched, then drew a single claw down the center, creating a small hole in my shorts.

He shoved the head of his cock into the hole. I rocked back further and listened to my pants tear completely down the center as he slid into me. My walls stretched around him, a cry of pain escaping my lips. His head wasn't even inside me yet, and it hurt.

Badly.

"Please, go slowly!" I whimpered. "I'm a virgin."

A vicious growl escaped his throat. "Even better."

Trying to distract myself from the pain, I moved my hands up and down the length of his horns. He grunted and continued to push himself into me, the pain slowly subsiding the faster I stroked his horn.

Another grunt, and he slammed himself balls deep into my pussy.

He peeled one of my hands off his horn and laid it across the enormous bulge inside my stomach that reached to my sternum. After pulling himself out of me and leaving me empty, he slammed himself into me again and filled me up, my stomach bulging so much that it nearly looked like I was pregnant.

My pussy tightened around his huge cock, the pressure building up and up in my core.

"I've never had a human take my cock so deep inside her," he growled, thrusting into my tight cunt. He seized my hips in his large hands and used me for his pleasure. "Devils, you take it so well. So fucking well."

I grabbed both of his horns again and stroked them faster, arching my spine and staring back into his dark eyes. He slithered out his forked tongue and slipped it into my mouth, curling it around mine.

He gripped my waist tighter, his thumb brushing over the head of his cock near my sternum. "Fuck," he groaned, wrapping his free hand around the base of his cock and balls and shoving himself even deeper into me. "Have to stick my heavy balls into you for good measure."

Another moan escaped my lips as I clenched around him.

"You're filled up with every inch of me," he growled. "Now you're going to beg."

"P-P-Please," I whined, gripping his horns tighter. "I want your cum."

"Tight-cunt virgins like you can never take any incubi's cum," he said. "It's nearly impossible to *not* fill you up past your cervix. Begging for an incubus like me to spray his cum into your hole is comparable to begging to get pregnant."

My pussy tightened even harder around him.

"If that's what you want," he slammed himself into me over and over and over, "then beg me to put a child inside you."

"P-P-Please!" I cried, unable to stop myself from moving my hips with his.

When he pulled out, I pushed my hips back so he wouldn't slip fully out of me. I wanted him buried as deep as he could go when his cum spilled into me. I wanted my belly full with all of his cum, with every last drop of it.

"Please," I pleaded. "Breed me!"

Like a vicious animal, he shook my hands off his horns, flattened me out on the bed, and lifted my hips high as possible into the air, ramming himself into me until I screamed out into the mattress. Wave after wave of pleasure rushed through me, my body trembling like it never had.

Then he stilled.

More pressure flooded through my pussy, and then—as if he felt the pressure too—he pulled out of me. His cum poured out of my pussy and onto the bed, creating a pool underneath me.

"Next time you summon a sex demon make sure you know what you're doing," he growled, resting his huge cock on my back as more of his cum leaked out of it. He swooped his fingers into the pool underneath me and slammed them back into my pussy. "Little innocent humans like you don't know how much you can truly take."

TRICK AND TREAT

"Trick or treat!" a group of five-year-olds dressed as superheroes shouted, holding out their plastic orange pumpkin buckets filled with candy. "Smell my feet! Give me something good to eat!"

I grabbed my bowl of candy on my side table, then crouched down to their levels and dropped a full-sized candy bar into each of their buckets. After they ran down my front walkway together, their parents waved and thanked me for them.

Smiling back, I stood up and watched them skip to the next house. My gaze drifted to a tall man dressed in a blue-gray janitor's jumpsuit and a completely white mask with a wooden ax in his hand.

He stared back from across the street, then turned away. I bit back a smirk. Cory was supposed to be over soon, and he had given me a glimpse of his costume that he planned to wear tonight over text: a picture of his veiny hand gripping an ax.

Was he teasing me tonight?

I shut the door and pressed my back against it, the heat growing between my thighs. Cory had just been a fling that I met up with a couple times a week–not someone who I'd actually consider dating–but damn did he have good dick.

Another knock came at the front door. I placed the bowl of candy down on the side table and straightened myself out, tucking some hair behind my ear and unbuttoning a button on my shirt to give myself a bit more cleavage.

When I pulled the door open, Cory stood outside with his head tilted to the side in that white mask of his. "Trick or treat," he said, his voice deep and gruff as he stepped into my house. He shut the door behind himself and ran the sharp edge of the ax up the column of my throat, then used it to lift my chin. "Give me something good to eat tonight, Blue."

A giggle escaped my lips at his nickname that he had given me when we were in high school. I gripped him by his janitor's jumpsuit and tugged him to the couch, falling back onto it and pulling him down with me.

We hadn't been sleeping together for that long, but this costume tonight was the sexiest thing he had ever worn over. Even sexier than all those damn suits he dressed in for work and those tight v-necks he had for the gym.

And to top it all off... I might've had a bit of a mask kink.

Getting fucked by a someone in a mask, not being able to see their face, sleeping with a man who might be the ugliest mother fucker alive... God, I didn't know why but it turned me the hell on. But it did.

Like usual, he slid his hands down my body and then in between my legs. I moaned and arched my back, spreading my thighs to give him better access. Halloween night was my favorite for many reasons.

This being one of them.

Instead of rubbing my clit like he usually did, he roughly grabbed my hips and ripped off my panties, forced me to rest my legs on his shoulders and buried his face between my thighs. He stuffed three long fingers into my mouth and lifted his mask enough to place his warm lips on my aching cunt.

"I guess I get a treat tonight too," I moaned.

He never ate my pussy.

His stubble tickled my inner thighs as he flicked his tongue against my clit. I arched my back as the pressure built inside of me, then I shoved a hand through his dark hair, a moan escaping my lips.

He held my hips in the air and shoved his fingers deeper into my mouth, making me gag and slobber all over them. He skillfully moved his tongue faster and harder until I squirmed underneath him. My legs trembled, and I squeezed my eyes closed.

I stared down at the masked man, teetering on the edge of an orgasm. With his free hand, he flicked my nipple through my shirt, and I lost complete control, loud moans escaping my mouth and my body flailing as an orgasm rippled through me.

"Oh, god," I moaned, gripping his hair and grinding my pussy against his face to pleasure myself. I didn't even believe in a higher being, but... "God. God. God. God. God. God. God!" I bucked my hips as my pussy pulsed and drooled all over his face.

After growling against my pussy, he pulled down his mask to cover his face and then tugged me into the air and on top of him so I straddled his waist. I curled my fingers into his shoulders, the pleasure still drifting through my body, and ground my pussy against the enormous bulge in his janitor's jumpsuit.

He reached between us, undid a zipper, and whipped out his dick. Once he seized my hips, he slammed me down onto him, his cock slipping into me and stretching me out more than it usually did.

He felt so big tonight that it actually... hurt a bit.

"Too big for you?" he asked, voice even more gruff.

I whined and tightened around him, still adjusting. He wrapped his arms underneath mine and gripped my shoulders, pulling me even further onto him until his balls were flush against my dripping pussy.

"T-T-Too m-much," I whimpered, trying to lift myself back off him.

For a moment, he resisted, but then he loosened his grip on me. I lifted myself up so six whole inches slipped out but three were still buried in my pussy, then I dropped back down onto him, threw my head back, and moaned.

"Holy... fuck!"

I bounced on his dick and stared into the empty mask eyes, my pussy tightening. The pressure rose in my core again, and I gripped his hair hard in my hand and tugged it back. Cory held my hips steady and pounded up into me, meeting me every time.

"Fuck," he grunted into his mask.

"P-Please, give me your cum," I begged.

Usually we used a condom, or I made Cory pull out, but I didn't give a damn tonight.

He shoved himself deep into me, spraying his cum into my tight hole. When he stilled, I couldn't help but let out another moan and come all over him. I sat down on him and lolled my head back, pleasure rushing through me.

God, this was the best fucking night of my life.

After I crawled off him, I walked to the bathroom to clean up because so much of his cum was gushing down my thighs. But when I heard the front door open, I grabbed the toilet paper roll, pulled up my underwear, and hurried out into the living room to see him walking out the front door.

Eyes wide, I hurried over to the door. "Where are you—"

Cory's car pulled up to the curb in front of my house. Dressed as some sort of Greek god with an ax, he shuffled out of his car and walked past whoever the hell had just been inside my house and... inside me. I swallowed hard as the man turned his head, lifted his mask up enough for me to see his lips, and smirked.

My heart pounded hard.

"Who was that?" Cory asked, walking into the house without even a kiss.

"I... I don't know," I whispered. "Some guy looking for candy."

"Isn't he a bit too old to be trick-or-treating?"

Gulping, I gripped the doorknob and pressed my thighs together to stop Cory from spotting the man's cum running down my legs. Heat gathered in my core, and I finally closed the door for the night.

I didn't know who the man was, but he knew my name. He had walked around my house like he had been inside it before. He had touched me like it hadn't been his first time, like he knew my body, my mind, me.

"Y-Yeah," I said, so Cory wouldn't ask questions.

How would I tell him that a random man had fucked me better than he ever had?

"Did you give him any?" Cory asked.

"I did," I whispered. "God, I did."

PUMPKIN SEED

CONTENT WARNING: MONSTER

The full moon glimmered in the sky on Halloween night. I rocked back on my heels and crossed my arms in an attempt to stay warm. My best friend had dragged me to this sexy costume party, dressed me in a bright fairy outfit, and then completely ditched me for some guy in wizard garb.

I sipped on my blood bag filled with red alcohol and tore my gaze away from the dark sky to the party that had trickled out into the surrounding forest. I locked eyes with a man who wore a pumpkin head lingering at the edge of the property.

With carved eyes that glowed a soft yellow, a wicked grin that stretched across the pumpkin ribs, and a bodybuilder's physique, he tilted his head back and poured the last few drops of his beer through the hollowed mouth hole.

After tossing the can into a black garbage bag, he glanced back at me and then walked into the woods, disappearing behind the thick fog. I gulped and straightened out my teal tutu that clinched my waist.

I shouldn't.

The heat grew between my thighs, and I pressed them together.

Fuck it. Shelly wouldn't be back anytime soon.

Once I placed my drink down, I walked around the dancing bodies toward the property's edge. The sounds of creatures growling, squealing, crying out for help on the speakers to create an eerie aura sent a shiver down my spine. But I stepped into the forest anyway.

I really shouldn't be doing this.

But my feet continued forward.

Had he even been looking at me?

Who cared? He was to fucking die for.

Ambling through the forest, I glanced around to find any trace of the guy.

Where did he go?

After a few more moments of searching, I let out a pitiful breath. What the hell was I even thinking following a man with a pumpkin head out into the forest during a full moon on Halloween night? I'd definitely be one of those dumb bitches who'd die if a serial killer ever chased after her with a knife.

I twirled around to head back and leaped up into the air when I spotted him standing inches from me, pumpkin head tilted downward, his wicked grin almost *smirking* at me now, and his abs... *God, his abs* were so close!

Swallowing hard, I stared up at him. "I–Uhm... I wasn't following you or... or anything."

Great, way to seem obvious about it.

Without saying a word, he stalked even closer to me.

My gaze traveled across his face. I didn't know how he did it, but the pumpkin looked like a real jack-o'-lantern with the flames inside and everything. And before I could even stop myself, I brushed my fingers against the ribs.

It was sorta-kinda sexy. Or maybe that was the alcohol talking.

He stepped closer to me and placed a single slender finger on my chin, lifting it.

"Why don't you take off your costume?" I whispered, confidence suddenly rushing through me. I didn't know where it had come from, but I was horny and aching for his cock now—anything to get my mind off being alone tonight.

I wouldn't care if it was a ghost or clown mask, but fucking with a whole pumpkin on his head might have been a bit too much. Wouldn't it get hot? Gross in there? It looked and felt like a real pumpkin; I could only imagine the seeds and goop still stuck to the sides against his cheek.

When he still didn't respond, nor attempt to remove the mask, I drew my tongue across my lips. I guess we could be anyone on Halloween night. And me? I wanted to be confident for once in my pathetic life.

So, I drew my fingers down his toned abdomen and slipped them underneath his waistband. I pressed my thighs together, my nipples hardening. God, he was so much bigger than I expected him to be. I could barely wrap my hand around his dick.

Moving closer to me, he dipped a hand between my legs and underneath my tutu. With skill, he brushed his fingers against my clit and rubbed it in small torturous circles. I stroked him faster, the pressure building inside me.

After I moaned softly, he massaged my salivating cunt faster. I clutched onto his cock and cried out as pleasure surged through me. My legs began shaking, and I toppled over onto my knees while riding out my orgasm.

He stood over me, the moonlight creating shadows across his taut abdomen. Heat gathered inside my core, and I stared up at the man with the pumpkin head as he pushed down his pants and whipped out his enormous cock that was almost too big to be human.

I wrapped both hands around the base and took his head into

my mouth, sliding my tongue around it. He laced a hand into my hair and tilted his head back, still not speaking a word to me, but a deep guttural grunt escaped his lips.

Pressing my thighs together, I sucked more of him into my mouth and bobbed my head. Every time I pulled back, I moved my hands up his shaft in a twisting motion, becoming more of a horny, desperate slut by the moment.

But it was Halloween night. Who cared?

When my spit covered his dick, I continued to stroke him and sucked his balls into my mouth, staring up at him through my lashes. He grunted again, the deep and feral sound sending shivers down my spine.

And then in one swoop, he wrapped his arms underneath the backs of my knees and lifted me into the air. I yelped and clutched his shoulders, waves of pleasure rushing through me. He pulled my panties underneath my tutu to the side and lined himself at my entrance.

"It's not going to fit," I whimpered, lounging in his arms. The backs of my knees were nestled in the crooks of his elbows, his biceps flexing against my inner thighs and making me warm in all the right places.

I rested my hands on his shoulders to hold myself up and stared down at his cock glistening with his precum against my entrance. I clenched and gazed back up at his soft yellow eyes. "It's too big," I whimpered.

He pushed his swollen head into my pussy anyway, stretching out my hole.

Inch by inch, he slipped deeper. Five inches in, he slammed the second half of himself into me. I screamed out in pleasure, my voice definitely traveling through these empty woods to the party. He gripped my ass cheeks and pulled them apart, thrusting quickly into me.

Pleasure rushed through me, clouding my mind. And when I

spotted an enormous black pointed tongue emerge from between his hollowed out mouth, I knew the alcohol had really settled into my system. Whatever they put in those drinks tonight really made people go wild.

He drew his tongue wildly back and forth across my neck, then buried his face between my breasts, sucking and kneading my nipples through my tank top, slobbering all over the thin material so anyone could see right through it.

I ran one hand across the back of his pumpkin head, pussy tightening. He continued driving into me, pounding faster with every motion. One last thrust, and he came deep inside my pussy.

I clutched onto his muscular shoulders, my rainbow-fairy colored nails digging into his skin, and threw my head back. A moan escaped my lips as pleasure rushed through my entire body, making my legs tremble in his arms.

Best damn Halloween of my life, and I hadn't even seen this guy's face.

After he pulled out of me, I leaned against the nearest tree and gazed between my legs. The thick liquid oozed down my thighs, leaving a trail of pumpkin seeds from my pussy to his throbbing orange cock.

Manhunt

Manhunt.

What started as a friendly game turned into a nightmare. We had signed up to play the biggest game of manhunt in the entire city. People came from all over the world for tonight, the night before Halloween, to run away from one designated *killer*.

But sometime along the way, this game took a sick turn. Instead of capturing people, this *killer* actually slaughtered every single one of the players.

Except me.

I pumped my legs as fast as they would go, my lungs burning, and glanced behind me as the man with the scarred up mask and a cleaver chased me. Filled with junk and trees and houses, the playing field went on forever and ever.

And the killer was approaching me quicker than I could sprint.

God, he is so fast. How is he so fast?

"Please," I cried, sprinting past some bloody corpses. "Please! Why are you doing this?" Tears streamed down my cheeks, but I couldn't stop them. I tried hard to conserve my energy, but I physically couldn't.

I would die here.

When I spotted a building, I ran into it and hoped to find somewhere to hide or escape him. I ran down an empty hallway, glanced behind me to see him turn the corner toward me, then I slipped into a room.

The room didn't have any doors, nor windows. And that's when I knew I was screwed.

I was fucking screwed!

He appeared at the door, threw my flailing body over his shoulder, and walked to a large thick hook that the organizers of this game placed around the game field. They must've thought these would be good decorations for Halloween.

Little did they know that this was *far* from great now.

I wiggled in his firm hold, but his bloody hands just gripped me tighter.

Instead of hooking me right through the chest and killing me instantly, he walked past the hook to a haystack feet away. I stared in horror as he deposited me on the hay, stepping back and watching me like a predator did with its prey.

Blood covered his throat, arms, and hands.

This was it.

This was where and how I'd die.

"If you're going to do it, do it already," I whispered. "Kill me."

"I've killed everyone for you," he said, voice deep and deadly. "You're my prize. That was the name of this game. That's what I paid to play as the killer. You're the only one that I ever wanted, the only player who put up a fight this entire match."

"You're crazy!" I seethed, spotting a knife he had attached to his belt. "Psychotic! Insane!"

I knew I had one chance. One fucking chance at survival tonight.

So, I grabbed it from his belt, my hands trembling.

I had never waved a knife at anyone before, had never felt the weight of a potential person's life in my hands. All I had to do was stuff the blade deep in this monster's throat and kill him dead. It should've been a simple decision for me; he had killed everyone else here.

This man was a cold-blooded killer.

This man killed my friends.

This man...

Why can't I do it? Why can't I kill him?

"You're not going to kill me," he said, wrapping his *palm* around the sharp edge of the knife and gripping it until he bled. He pulled it away from me. "You're not a monster, like I am, Willow."

"H-how do you know my name?" I whispered, fear striking me right through my bones.

When he removed his mask, my eyes widened. It wasn't just anyone running after the entire group of victims, but a man who looked normal, like a regular person I'd see walking down the city streets, a guy who'd flash me a sweet smile.

After pulling the knife completely from my hands, he gripped it by the handle and drew it up the side of my neck. I froze, but my body trembled slightly, the feel of metal against me making me shiver.

"Will you let me out?" I whimpered, tears pouring down my cheeks. "Please, let me out."

"All their deaths are on your hands. And all their blood..." He drew his tongue up the column of my neck and grinned wickedly against my skin. "...is all over your body now. You'll never escape, Willow, even next year when I pay a billion dollars to hunt you again."

When he slid the blade across my neck, I flinched. My heart was racing against my chest, and I sucked in a sharp breath. The blade didn't enter me, but the thought of it slipping inside my flesh was making me sick to my stomach.

"What-What are you doing? Can you stop? Please, I'll do anything. What do you want?"

He smirked down at me, his grin evil and menacing. "The only thing I want is you."

"Me?" I whispered, my voice trembling. The psycho stared down at me with the devil in his black eyes. "But... I... I don't understand, why are you doing this? Why me? Why did you hunt us? Why didn't--"

Before I could finish, he dropped the knife and cleaver, grasped my hips, and lifted me into the air. Once he leaped onto the hay barrel, he sat me on top of him so I straddled his waist.

A thin layer of sweat covered his huge, muscular forearms. No wonder why he had the endurance to hunt down hundreds of people and kill them tonight, and *still* have energy for me. He was fucking ripped. And underneath me... his cock was rock hard against my shorts.

I clenched.

I fucking clenched.

And he felt it. He gripped my hips and forced them down onto him. The head of his cock was pressing against my entrance. I tightened again and stared into his eyes with my wavering ones.

"Please, please stop. What are you doing?"

He placed his bloody hands all over me sliding them up my thighs and around my waist, pulling me closer and closer and closer to him. He was a psychopath, a pure evil psychopath. My body was reacting to him naturally, and I couldn't stop it.

With one hand holding me in place, he grabbed the knife and cut my shorts off my body, leaving me bare to him. He threw the material to the side, then took my hand and wrapped it around the handle of the knife, putting his larger hand over mine.

After forcing me to cut the front of his pants until his cock sprang out of them, I released the knife. He set it to the side, completely trusting me not to pick it back up and stab him over and over. After everything that happened tonight, I should've.

I fucking should've.

He watched me as he positioned himself at my entrance. I clenched and held back a whimper, staring down at the man who had blood covering so much of his body from the hundreds of people he killed tonight.

When he thrust into me for the first time, I pressed my lips together to suppress a moan. I didn't want him to know how much I enjoyed this because I shouldn't be enjoying this. Not at all. This was torture. Pure, agonizing torture.

After what he did to my friends, after what he did to everyone here, after the blood and the mess, I fucking enjoyed this. I was sick.

Once he placed his hands on my shoulders, he pumped into me. His thrusts were agonizingly slow at first until they became quicker and rougher as if he was claiming my insides like they belonged to him.

My pussy tightened around his throbbing cock. I squeezed my eyes closed and tried hard to get myself to come down. I didn't want to come because of him, but I couldn't get myself to stop. It felt... it felt... God, it felt good.

I couldn't stop myself from gripping hard onto his shoulders and riding his cock. He stopped pumping into me, his hands all over my ass, helping me ride him, helping me ride the fucking monster.

"You're going to come for me," he said.

I swallowed hard and shook my head. No, I couldn't.

"Yes," he said, staring up at me with fascination. "You are. Your body is stiffening, your pussy tightening harder every moment."

"I'm not going to come for–"

He seized my nipples and tugged on them. My words turned into moans, as pleasure exploded through my body. My pussy pulsed around his cock over and over, the ecstasy more incredible than I had ever experienced it.

Once I stopped bouncing, he buried his cock deep into my pussy and groaned in pleasure. My pussy pulsed more around his length, milking out every single ounce of this killer's cum.

When he finally pulled out of me, he set me on the haystack and grabbed the cleaver. "I look forward to next year, Willow. Whether or not you join next year's game, I will hunt you down and have you again."

TO READ PART 2, sign up for Emilia's newsletter!

HAUNTED HOUSE

Standing at the bottom of my gravel driveway, I placed my hands on my hips, rocked back on my heels, and beamed at this mansion that was now *mine*. It cost me exactly one thousand dollars for this house, a freaking *steal* in this area. Most two-story, five-bedroom houses neared a million in downtown Durnbone.

Sure, I had to clean it up a bit, get rid of the boarded-up windows and the eerie fog that hovered near the bottom of the house. But it was fine. It wouldn't take me *that* long to do it. A couple weeks of cleaning non-stop, and I'd have the sexiest damn place in the neighborhood.

"You live here?" a girl asked, riding her baby blue bike down the street toward me. She *skrrt*-ed to a stop right before her front wheel could touch the driveway, almost as if she was terrified of what would happen if it did, then re-adjusted her pink helmet. "My mommy says that ghosts live there!"

I crouched down to her level and smiled. "There is no such thing."

"Yeah, there is! Mommy said she saw one in the window."

After glancing back at the house, I examined all the wood

covering the windows. I didn't understand why everyone was so worked up over this place. Even when I went to the realtor, she warned me to stay away.

But ghosts weren't real.

The house might've *looked* haunted with a full moon shining behind it, illuminating the grotesque and bare trees, thick fog heavy from below, but it was nothing, and I'd prove it to the entire neighborhood one day.

"Actually…" I turned back to the young girl and tapped my finger on her bike's bell, making it chime through the dusk. "I heard the ghosts come out at night, when the moon is full and monsters are hungry to devour little children bite by bite."

Stricken back in fear, she pointed to the house. "B-but i-it is full."

"You better get going then, before the ghosts get you too."

Eyes widening, she twisted her bike around, started pumping her little legs, and disappeared down the road. Giggling to myself, I walked up the driveway, through the overgrown lawn, and to the front door that had a *keep out* sign stapled to it.

I pulled out my key and blew out a breath, opening the doors to the house that was *mine* for the first time ever. I probably should've requested a tour, but I wanted to snatch this place up before anyone else bought it and, besides, the realtor had told me from the beginning she didn't give tours in houses like this.

The house was a filthy mess with black footprints and hand-prints decorating the black-and-white checkered floor and yellow walls, *Get out* etched onto the back of the front door, and fallen glass literally everywhere. Shutting the door behind me, I glanced around, listening to the light hum of something.

And, suddenly, the noise ceased, a deafening silence falling over the house.

Knowing that it was just my imagination, I walked further down the hallway and turned on a flickering light. I wasn't sure how the electricity stayed on all these years, but someone was paying it apparently, though the light bulbs needed to be replaced. And this floor, *ugh*, it would take days to make it a shiny, glistening white again.

After walking up the creaking steps, I wandered down the dimly lit hallway and toward a bedroom door. Like magic, the door opened for me. I stopped dead in my tracks, heart racing, and shook my head. It was just the wind blowing in from an open window somewhere in this house. Nothing more.

I wasn't about to let those rumors get to me.

Instead of freaking out, I stepped into the room.

See, nothin—

The door slammed behind me, and I jumped back in fear, breath catching in the back of my throat. I glanced over my shoulder, expecting to see some looming white ghost or those twin girls from that horror movie, but I saw nothing. Absolutely nothing.

Tree branches scraped against the window, creating a grotesque pattern through the messed up and ruined blinds. I swallowed my terror and moved further into the room toward the made-up bed where there were a couple—what seemed to be—indents, as if before the previous owners left, they had sat in these exact spots.

But that was years upon years ago.

Surely, those indents wouldn't still be there, right?

What was I even thinking? I was working myself up over nothing at all.

I sat down on the bed, immediately jumping back up when I felt something other than a mattress under me. But when I went to move away, someone wrapped their arms around my waist and pulled me back down onto the bed or onto... whatever it was under me. It kind of felt like... legs. Except there wasn't anything but a mattress. I was sure of it.

Though... when I glanced back at the door to see the lock twist all by itself, I knew I was in deep shit.

The hum of voices drifted through the air again and interrupted the deafening silence. What felt like hands and fingers drifted around my waist and up my abdomen, strands of my hair floating in the air all by itself. I sucked in a breath, grasping the hair to pull it back down but it still moved on its own.

"What's going on?" I asked, voice tight with fear. "Is someone there?"

Hands moved up and down my body, fingers curling around the hems of my shirt, pulling it in three different directions. I stayed still, unable to move from the firm grip around my waist. The legs under me shifted, so that I straddled the thigh grinding up into me and making me warm in so many sinful places.

I squeezed my eyes closed, my nipples hardening as my shirt was ripped apart and pulled down completely, my breasts falling out of it. "It's just my imagination. It's just my imagination. It's just my imagination."

When I open my eyes, everything will be back to normal.

But when I reopened my eyes, my jeans were unbuckled and something was fondling my pussy, the impression of a hand pressed against my cloth panties. I let out a piercing scream until someone slapped a hand over my mouth and pulled me back onto the bed; the fingers moving faster against my clit.

"You're ours now," someone whispered into my ear.

Both oddly enjoying this and freaking out, I squirmed in his hold. The pressure rose in my core, the fingers moving even faster around my clit in tortuous little circles. Someone squeezed my nipples, and I moaned—*fucking moaned*—as wave after wave of pleasure rushed through my entire body.

I curled my toes and whimpered, my body finally relaxing against the ghost underneath me. Pussy tingling in all the right ways, I pulled my legs together to displace the intense pleasure pumping through me.

"Who are you? Who is *us*?" I said in a breathy whisper.

But instead of answering me, one picked me up and placed me onto the bed on all fours, tugging down my jeans and underwear and ripping off the rest of my shirt. The bed dipped in front of me, what seemed to be knees indenting the sheets. Someone cupped my chin, placed something at my lips, and rammed it into me, almost immediately hitting the back of my throat.

I gagged on the cock, spit running down my chin, and glanced over into the rusty bedroom mirror to see the indent of a huge cock in my throat, bigger than I'd ever seen before, something two times the size—both in girth and in length—compared to any guy I'd ever been with.

The good kind of tears welled up in my eyes, my throat closing around the dick. I curled my fingers around the bedsheets and moaned out, my pussy clenching. From behind, someone grabbed my hips and rubbed their dick against my entrance, pushing it inside of me. I threw my head back, the cock falling out of my mouth and slapping against what sounded like a thigh.

"Oh my god," I moaned, being touched by what seemed to be a dozen hands.

Nipples tugged. Clit rubbed. Ass smacked and grabbed and pulled apart. This felt too good to be freaking real. The pressure was driving me higher and higher and higher. Ghosts were pulling out and pushing into all my holes, slapping their dicks against my tits and making them sway.

"More," I whispered. "Give me mo—"

Someone thrust a cock back into my mouth, filling me up. Two others lifted my hands and made me wrap them around themselves, stroking. The hum of voices became louder and louder with every passing second. And then something warm filled my throat.

When the ghost pulled out of me, I found my head dropping and his cum dripping out of me and onto the sheets. I gasped for air and glanced up, brows drawn together. "That was it?" I asked, desperate for more.

I didn't know what it was, but I had never felt better than this.

And, before I knew it, another ghost pushed themselves inside of my mouth, their hand wrapping around the front of my tight throat. Someone brushed their nose against my ear, their lips following. *"We've lived here alone for twelve years. You're trapped here until we're done using you."*

To read Part 2, sign up for Emilia's newsletter!

MORE CONTENT

Want more one shots? Emilia writes steamy one shots every single Wednesday on her Patreon!

As a supporter, you also receive the benefit of voting on the next book that Emilia writes as well as downloads to her previously published content.

Also By

Contemporary Romance

Stepbrother

Poison

The Bad Boy

Detention

Excite Me

Paranormal Romance

Submitting to the Alpha

Come Here, Kitten

Alpha Maddox

My Werewolf Professor

The Twins

Four Masked Wolves

Monster Lover

Erotica

Climax: Erotic One-Shot Collection

About the Author

Emilia Rose is a USA Today best-selling author of steamy romance. Highly inspired by her study abroad trip to Greece in 2019, Emilia loves to include Greek and Roman mythology in her writing.

She graduated from the University of Pittsburgh with a degree in psychology and a minor in creative writing in 2020 and now writes novels as her day job.

With over 18 million combined book views online and a growing presence on reading apps, she hopes to inspire other young novelists with her tales of growth and imagination, so they go on to write the stories that need to be told.

Join Emilia's newsletter for exclusive giveaways, early chapter releases, and more!

PRINT BOOKS

SCAN THE QR CODE WITH YOUR PHONE TO VIEW ALL OF EMILIA'S BOOKS!